The Barrier

India in the 1890s . . . the heyday of the British Raj . . . the circumscribed life of a military hill-station. Against this vivid background *The Barrier* sets the scene of an explosive love story which simmers beneath the surface of rigid social convention. A British Colonel brings a young girl to India, straight from an English farm, and marries her. Unhappy in her marriage, she falls in love with one of her husband's servants—an Indian boy who acts as her groom when she goes riding each day. It is only through her poetry that she is able to express the love that consumes her.

ROBIN MAUGHAM

The Barrier

A novel containing five sonnets by
JOHN BETJEMAN
written in the style of the period

W. H. ALLEN
LONDON AND NEW YORK
A division of Howard & Wyndham Ltd
1973

PRINTED AND BOUND IN GREAT BRITAIN BY BUTLER AND TANNER LTD,
LONDON AND FROME, FOR THE PUBLISHERS,
W. H. ALLEN & CO. LTD, 43 ESSEX STREET, LONDON WC2R 3JG.
ISBN 0 491 00853 8

Author's Note

When I first had the idea for this novel, I realised that it was essential to have five sonnets. So I went to see my friend John Betjeman and gave him a full outline of the plot. After he had read it, he agreed to write the five sonnets in the style of the period. I am extremely grateful to him.

I went to Ootacamund—a hill-station in the Niligini Mountains in Southern India. I spent several months taking notes, for I discovered—to my pleasure—that the place had scarcely changed in eighty years. Telacamund in my novel bears a certain resemblance to Ootacamund. But, in fact, the village and the district are fictional as are all the characters in the novel.

R. M.

For William

With thanks,

R. M.

I

Beneath our windows I can hear the crows cawing in the stableyard. The door leading to Tom's dressing-room is open, and I can see him standing in front of a cheval-glass, shaving himself. He wears only a pair of drill trousers which fit tightly round his narrow waist. The muscles slide on his thick shoulders. He told me that he placed the looking-glass in that position so he could occasionally glance down into the yard of the compound to make sure the grooms—or syces as I must learn to call them—and the sweepers were working properly. Now and again he turns towards our bed in the next room, and then I pretend to be asleep, for if at this instant he speaks to me I shall not know what to answer. I feel like an actress who has not learned her part. Yesterday, and every day before, it was different. When we first met, I was more spontaneous with Tom than I could be with other people—even with my parents. As a child, I had worshipped him when he came to visit us; as a girl, I loved him; but now, as a young woman—for now that I am married I can no longer think of myself as a girl—now that I am a wife I do not understand my role.

Why did none of them explain to me? What good were their hints and elusive warnings? Why did they pretend to me that after my wedding night I would awake a different person? Why did they allow me to believe that the act of love, 'the moment when two bodies become one flesh', as my mother put it, would lift my heart in ecstasy and send my spirit soaring to the sky? Or were they right in their belief, and have I somehow been to blame?

I

When Tom joined me in bed last night, our very first night together, he was gentle. As he lay against me, his hands began to move softly along my body and reached my breasts. And I thought: this is how it will begin. Quite soon the moment will come. Then he took my hands and made me caress him, and I could feel the firmness of his neck and the strength of his shoulders and, later, the strange contrasts of rough and smooth in the texture of his skin. And for a moment I did indeed feel transformed by joy as I pressed my lips against him. Suddenly he shuddered and his body became rigid. His hands as they took hold of me were no longer tender. He was breathing quickly. His light brown eyes were staring at me, but he was not seeing me. It was as if he were gazing at some distant vision he had seen before, but had never reached. He drew back and grasped me so roughly that I winced. Then came the stab of pain, a pain which grew to agony as he pressed down on me. His hands were now clasping my skin. I could not escape his frenzy. I felt that my whole body would be pierced until I bled to death. I must have cried out, for his hand covered my mouth. For an instant he drew back, and I believed the worst of the pain was finished. But then he lurched forward. As he lurched, the pain seemed to invade my whole being. He began to move rapidly. His thrusts were now carefully defined as if he wished to discover each new place in me that he could hurt. He was panting. The thrusts grew quicker. Then his body was convulsed in a fierce surge of force. The arm holding me clutched at my skin like an animal. Then he gave a sigh, as if he too were in anguish. And it was finished.

The crows are still cawing outside our bedroom. I will turn back my mind to the past to forget my throbbing pain.

<hr />

I enjoyed the long journey from England to Madras. I didn't mind the occasional discomfort; I loved watching the waves dashing against the hull of the steamship and enjoyed the warm heat of the Indian Ocean, the flying fish and the dolphins. I liked many of the passengers, and was amused by the gallantry affected by the young officers returning to India from leave. Tom's sister, Margaret, in her capacity of chaperon, was displeased by my friendliness towards them all. 'As the future wife of a Colonel,' she told me, 'you must learn to be more reserved.' I had of course long since realised that Margaret, daughter of a baronet, was convinced that the daughter of a tenant farmer was very lucky to be engaged to her brother. I knew it. In fact, I was amazed when he proposed to me.

I had known Tom since I was a child. Sometimes, on his way back from a ride round the estate, he would stop at our house for a drink with my father. Even in those days I was attracted to him. I would clamber on to his knees and he would hand me a piece of biscuit soaked in wine. My father would laugh. 'You'll make a drunkard of her,' he'd say—I think he was proud of his friendship with the son of his landlord—and I would nibble my biscuit and lie back against Tom's chest, feeling the warmth that came from his body. I remember I was fascinated by the dark hairs that grew on the back of his hands. I was nine years old when Tom rejoined his regiment in India.

He came back on leave when I was fifteen. I saw him ride up to our house as I was sitting on the swing my parents had put up for me. He was now far leaner, and his skin was a tawny colour, but I recognised him from far away, and without thinking I ran across the lawn to greet him. For a moment he stared at me in astonishment. Then he laughed.

'At first I didn't know who you were,' he said. 'You've quite grown up, haven't you?'

'You've grown thinner,' I replied.

He was silent. He was still staring at me with his hazel-coloured eyes. Suddenly he leaned down towards me and stroked my cheek. I didn't move. His hand slid round to my neck. I could feel the heat of his fingers as they pressed against my skin. I stood motionless.

'You like me, don't you?' he said.

I nodded. Hidden by my hair, his hand was now caressing me. I couldn't speak.

'Do you think you could love me?' he asked.

Again I nodded. I wanted to take his other hand and kiss

the hairs on the back of it. But I was afraid my parents might be watching. His hand felt heavy against me.

'Shall I tell you a secret?' he asked quietly.

'Yes,' I answered.

'Do you promise you'll keep the secret?'

'Of course I will,' I replied.

His face now looked stern and angry, as if I had said something to annoy him.

'Well, it's this,' he said, glaring. 'In a few years' time, when I next get leave, I shall come home and I hope we shall love each other.'

That evening as I lay in bed I wondered if I had mistaken Tom's words or dreamed them. But I could still feel the weight of his hand on my shoulder, and I could remember the intentness with which he had glared at me, as if his eyes resented each word that his voice had spoken. But the words had been said—that was the important fact. And I was in love with him. So what else could I do but wait?

I was an only child. My mother was sometimes laid up in bed with various ailments. Gradually I took over the arrangement of our small household. I was busy. But I still found time to read. I had enjoyed reading since I was a child. I now began to take down stray volumes of poetry from my father's bookcase. I became enthralled. I read more. Presently I discovered that lines of poetry would slide into my mind, and I would write them down. Soon I started to write sonnets. I have never shown my poetry to anyone; I doubt if I ever shall. I write for myself.

In addition to the books of poetry (Byron and Keats were my favourites) I now began to read books about India, and immediately I was fascinated. The country itself offered amazing contrasts between steaming jungles and ice-cold mountains, between bleak deserts and scented gardens. The people varied from the hawk-faced lean Pathans in the north to the prune-black Tamils in the south. Fierce racial hatred existed between Hindus and Moslems, and the country was further divided by an elaborate system of castes. Famine and disease were spread over the whole land. We, the British, had acquired India by conquest. Our country had taken over the moral responsibility of ruling this vast continent which was now a part of our Empire. That responsibility, it seemed, could only be maintained by force. The many regiments of Indian soldiers led by British officers were part of that force. Tom, who had now become Colonel of his regiment, was a symbol of our determination to overcome the evil intrigues of ambitious or corrupt natives and to unite all of India under a humane and powerful administration. The Viceroy had declared that in India was to be found 'the true fulcrum of dominion, the real touchstone of our Imperial greatness or failure'.

———◆◆◆———

As he had done before, Tom left his sister Margaret to look after his property in India, when he returned on leave for the second time. She was some five years older than he was. The day after Tom's return to England he rode across to our house. I was in the garden, picking some flowers to put on the dining-room table.

I was almost nineteen years old. Tom saw me. He dismounted quickly, tethered his horse, and strode towards me. I put down the flowers. I could feel the beats of my heart. I stood there in silence. Tom did not speak. He took hold of my hands and grasped them. He pointed to a bench at the end of the lawn.

'Anne,' he said to me. 'Wait there. I only hope I won't be long.'

Then he turned and walked towards the house and rang the bell. While I waited I tried to examine my emotions. I was still in love with him. He was my hero, and now there was a hope that he would be my husband. He was over twice my age. But what did I care? He was strong and healthy. He seemed to exude an odd vitality which affected everyone he met. His vigour seemed inexhaustible. He was tall and handsome, with his keen face and thick moustache. And I loved him very much.

At last the door of the house opened and Tom came out. He walked straight to the bench where I was sitting. He knelt down beside me on the lawn.

'I have asked your parents for their permission for me to propose marriage to you,' he said. 'They have consented.'

He paused. His voice was hoarse and he cleared his throat.

'Anne,' he said, 'please will you marry me?'

He was still kneeling. I stretched out my arms and touched the dark hairs on the back of his wrists.

'Yes,' I said. 'I love you and I will marry you.'

He rose. He kissed my forehead, my cheeks and my mouth. Then suddenly he drew away. He took my right hand and bent down and brushed it with his lips. It was a cold, formal gesture.

'I shall do my best to make you a good husband,' he said. 'I shall try to make you happy. I think you will soon grow accustomed to life in India.'

Then he bowed to me politely.

'I have invited you and your father and mother to dine with my parents tonight. At dinner our engagement will be formally announced.'

Once again he bowed, turned away, crossed the lawn, untethered his horse and rode off.

A few months later Tom's sister, Margaret, tall, thin, pale and stern, arrived in England to help me buy my trousseau and to chaperon me on the journey to India. My mother was too unwell to face the voyage; my father would not leave her, so no one from my family would be present at my wedding.

———◆◆◆———

Tom met the ship in Madras. We stayed two days in the oven-like heat which—to Margaret's annoyance—I rather enjoyed. Then we began the journey to Telacamund, seven thousand feet above sea-level in a mountain range in the South of India. Here stands the hill-station to which Tom takes his regiment during the hot season down on the plain. Our luggage was stowed away in the bottom of the covered bullock waggons; boards were laid over our valises; our bedding was placed on top of the boards, so that when we or the horses we rode grew tired, we could lie flat in the little carts while they jolted along the parched plain. As the road twisted higher and higher above a steaming jungle, the air began to grow more fresh. There were fewer villages and fewer water-buffalo. We could smell timber and see outcrops of rock, goats and white-humped cattle, and, in the distance, dark forests of fir. Swarms of monkeys played in the branches of huge cedar trees. Mossy rocks rose from streams flanked by ferns and flowers. Creepers dripped from the pines. Presently, grass-covered hills appeared and, on the next stage of our journey, stretches of downs rolled away to the horizon under a clear sky.

It was dark when we reached Telacamund a day later. First, we rode towards Tom's house on the hillside above the native village. The night was cold. Clouds had covered the stars. I could see little of the compound we entered, but lamps were alight in the porte-cochère of Mickleden—a large two-storeyed building nearly a hundred years old. We entered a house which might well have belonged to our own home counties except for the elephant-tusks on the side-table in the hall and a profusion of Benares brass trays and Kashmir carpets. A fire burned in the drawing-room with its chintz-covered chairs and solid English furniture.

'It's so deliciously cold up in these hills that we have a fire lit in all the rooms in the evenings,' Tom told me. 'It's strange to see fires burning in the month of May.'

Two Indian servants brought tea and cake for Margaret and me, and a whisky for Tom. Then we drove in Tom's carriage to the little hotel which had just been built and where I was to stay with Margaret until I was married to Tom in a week's time. In my small bedroom there was another log-fire crackling and all the usual furniture of an English household.

In the morning I drew back the curtains, opened wide the window and looked out, and I was amazed. Spread out before me was a long lawn flanked by herbaceous borders. I was staring at an English garden, full of roses and irises, geraniums and stocks, lupins and primroses. Fat shining black crows waddled, cawing, across the immaculately kept lawn.

Only the fantastic bright flashing colours of some bird swooping above the compound wall reminded me that I was in a foreign land. As the mist lifted I could see to the west a lake partly surrounded by a thick forest, and to the east in the far distance on the gentle slope of a long hill, I saw neat rows of barrack-huts and a barrack square, dominated by a grandstand. All around me villas and bungalows nestled in well-kept gardens.

———————◆◆◆◆———————

Yesterday—already it seems like many weeks ago—I was married to Tom by the Vicar of Telacamund, assisted by the regiment's chaplain. Once again we might have been in England. Light filtered through the stained glass windows on to pleasantly carved oak pews in the beautiful English church, built in early Victorian gothic in the first decade of the century. In their full-dress uniform the officers, escorting their wives who had put on their best finery for the occasion, looked very neat and very English. Only the jet-black faces of the Missionary boys and girls in the choir reminded me that we were in India. I could not make myself aware that the most important event in my life was now taking place. The first chord of Mendelssohn's Wedding March which was blared out suddenly by the regimental band drawn up in the churchyard brought me to reality. I was married; I was walking down the aisle on Tom's arm. I was passing beneath an arch of swords; walking beside the smart scarlet tunics of the band of Indian soldiers; I was moving through the graveyard where ferns and moss clung to the worn headstones, advancing beneath tall cypresses towards the lych-gate where the carriage awaited to take us home.

And now I am lying in our marriage-bed, watching Tom at his cheval-glass through half-closed eyes, listening to the ceaseless cawing of the crows in the compound, wondering what I shall say when Tom turns round to me, wondering if I shall ever be able to learn my role.

2

Automatically, as I always do when I come into the dining-room, I made certain that the dishes had been laid out in order on the hot-plates and that the silver was well polished. I helped myself to a slice of paw-paw, and, without thinking, pulled back my chair at the head of the table. Then I remembered. I put the chair back in its place and seated myself in a position half-way between the high-backed mahogany chairs which belonged to father and which now stand at either end of the table. I realised that Tom and Anne would be late; I was hungry, so I began eating. Yet as soon as I began eating, I found I had no appetite. I felt curiously uneasy and listless. Perhaps the arrangements for the wedding had tired me more than I supposed. Perhaps I was worried.

Though I had always been aware that it was almost inevitable that my brother would one day marry, I had put the notion firmly at the back of my mind. Tom seemed content with his life; I was there to look after his household; he flirted with some of the girls he met, but he never seemed really interested in any particular one of them. How could I guess that he had determined to marry the daughter of one of father's tenant-farmers at Newcombe? I had never even met the girl. I knew that Tom sometimes called at the Wicksons' house on his rides round the estate. Father had mentioned it in one of his letters to me. But until Tom came back from his recent leave and told me he was engaged to be married I had never known the reason for his interest in the Wickson family. I confess I was hurt that Tom had not told me sooner. Since Tom and I were children we have almost always shared our secrets. If I had found out earlier about his love for the girl I doubt if I would have tried in any way to persuade Tom against proposing to her, but at least I could have pointed out to him tactfully that the marriage was rather unsuitable. After all, when father dies Tom will inherit the baronetcy, and I had hoped that if indeed he did marry, he would marry into a family of some distinction. However, Tom made his proposal public before I had even heard about it. The girl is obviously besotted about him. Let us hope she will make him a good wife. But I must confess I am beginning to doubt it. Beneath that fair hair and soft skin, behind those lively blue eyes she is self-opinionated and, I suspect, obstinate. She is quite clever and observant—I grant her that. But recently while in England she has read a lot of books about India, many of them by writers who formed their bigoted opinions after a brief and superficial tour of the country. She has absorbed these new-fangled views, and little that I can say can change her mind. One can only hope she will learn the truth before she offends our friends out here with her callow talk about educating the natives or building vast hospitals for the poor.

As I was sitting half-way down the empty table finishing my cup of tea, Kumar, our head bearer, came in. With his long scarlet tunic and the broad yellow sash round his waist and his green turban he always looks as smart as if he were on parade. Yet I do not altogether trust him. I feel there is something unpleasant about him. However, he is clean and efficient. As usual, he carried the menu-book for the day with him, and our usual ritual began.

'Good-morning, Kumar,' I said.

'Good-morning, Memsahib,' he said, and grinned obsequiously as he handed me the menu-book.

I turned over the pages; the familiar dishes flickered before my eyes.

'Now, let's see,' I began. 'The Colonel will be here for lunch, so we'll be three.'

Kumar nodded solemnly as if blessing the new arrival.

'Curried eggs and roast chicken,' I said. 'For dessert we'll have a sherry trifle.' Then I remembered that Anne liked plenty of sugar with a trifle. 'Put in more sugar than usual,' I added. 'The new Memsahib likes puddings sweet.'

Kumar salaamed to me and left the room.

It was at luncheon that Anne made her first obvious gaffe. She was sitting in her new place at the head of the table. Kumar was standing a few paces behind her. Belur, a fat Tamil of thirty, rather self-conscious in his newly-starched tunic and new white gloves, was handing round the trifle. Without thinking he first handed the dish to me.

'No, Belur,' I said. 'I told you to hand dishes to the new Memsahib first.'

'Aama, Memsahib,' Belur said, and took the dish across to Anne who was looking very wan at the top of the table.

To my amazement, Anne turned round in her chair and smiled up at Belur. 'I'm sorry, Belur,' Anne said, still smiling at the bearer. 'I'm afraid I couldn't eat another morsel.'

Tom frowned at her. There was silence while Belur handed the trifle to me and to Tom.

'I had the pudding made extra sweet,' I explained, 'because I know you like sweet things.'

'I do. I do indeed,' Anne answered. 'But to tell the truth, I'm not very hungry.'

'Perhaps the curried eggs disagreed with her,' I said to Tom.

Tom laughed—I always love the sound of his laughter. Then he looked towards his wife, and at that moment I could see how much he adored her. 'Anne will soon get used to curry,' he said gently. Then he turned back to me. 'Meanwhile,' he continued, 'hurry up the coffee, will you, Margaret. I've got a parade at three.'

I rang the bell which I had placed at my side of the table.

'In this heat?' Anne asked Tom.

'Heat! This is nothing,' Tom replied. 'Down on the plain we parade them when the thermometer's well over ninety.'

'Why?' Anne asked.

Tom smiled at her. 'Because my regiment is composed of fighting soldiers,' he explained. 'And they must learn to fight under any conditions.'

'When will you be back?' Anne asked.

'In time for supper.'

'I thought it was a Mess-night,' I said.

'It was,' Tom answered. 'But I managed to get it postponed. I wanted to spend my second night as a married man having a quiet supper at home.' Once again, Tom smiled at Anne. 'I'll get away as soon as I can,' Tom continued, still gazing at his bride. 'Why don't you go for a ride in the late afternoon when it's cooler?'

For an instant I thought that Tom had forgotten my bad fall during the jackal-hunt four months ago. 'I can't ride since my accident,' I told Anne. 'And you can't possibly go out alone. That's certain.'

'We can send out a syce with her,' Tom said. 'She can ride Cara. With a groom she'll be safe.'

Cara was a lightly-built high-spirited young mare that Tom had bought from a fellow-officer who was in debt.

'Cara can be difficult,' I warned.

'Anne has ridden since she could walk,' Tom answered.

Kumar came in and handed round the coffee on a silver tray, and then went out.

'Well, it's your responsibility,' I told my brother. Then I turned back to Anne. 'In any case, I planned to take you for a drive this afternoon,' I said.

'Are you sure there's nothing I could do to help about the house?' Anne asked.

'We have three bearers, two cooks, three ayahs, five sweepers and four gardeners,' I explained to her gently. 'Quite apart from two dhobis for the washing, two water-carriers, a cowman, and three watchmen. And I superintend them all. So it's very kind of you, Anne, but I don't really see quite what you could do.'

Anne stared at me. With her straw-coloured hair and vivid blue eyes, with her expression of innocence combined with an odd look of yearning, I could see why a man like Tom should be attracted to her.

'Does this house need so many servants?' Anne asked.

'I can assure you that it's the normal staff establishment for someone in Tom's position,' I replied.

'Besides,' Tom said, 'servants out here cost less than the booze we drink.'

For a while there was silence.

'Perhaps I could go out riding after our drive?' Anne asked.

'Of course you can,' Tom answered as he finished his coffee. 'But don't go too far into the hills. There are panthers in the hills.' And he walked out.

———◆◆◆———

First, Anne and I drove to the library, because Anne had now become a member and she wanted to take out some books about the neighbourhood and an anthology of poetry. The library had been built in about 1800. Outside, with its wide lawn and tall cedars, with its white pilasters and pediment over the stone façade, and its long windows, the place looked quite impressive, but inside I found it gloomy. The dark corridors were lined with even darker books; the walls were streaked with damp; and there was an unpleasant musty smell. However, Anne seemed to like its interior, for I had to wait in the open carriage for quite a time before she came out with three books under each arm.

'The librarian was most kind and helpful,' Anne announced.

'I thought he was away ill.'

'No. He seemed in perfect health.'

'You can't mean,' I began, 'you can't mean the Indian clerk?'

'He was Indian,' Anne replied.

'That was the librarian's clerk,' I told her. 'You don't have to have anything much to do with that horrid little man. You just tell him the books you want and let him go and fetch them.'

Anne was silent as we drove towards the Botanical Gardens, inaugurated to celebrate our Queen's Jubilee. Anne had not as yet visited them.

'I expect it must seem strange to you out here,' I said to Anne presently.

'A little.'

I took in a breath. 'I hope you won't mind me offering you a word of advice,' I said.

'Please do,' Anne answered.

'Don't be too familiar with the servants.'

'Familiar?'

'There was no need to explain to Belur at lunch today *why* you didn't want any trifle, and then to say you were sorry,' I told her. 'Just shake your head, and he'll serve the next person. Please try to understand. Apart from the Rajah—with whom we have to keep in for political reasons—we just don't mix with the Indians. It's not done. Do you understand?'

'Yes,' Anne said. 'I understand.'

The way from the library to the Jubilee Gardens lay through the village. I had not yet taken Anne to the village; I wanted her first to become at least a little accustomed to life in India. But this afternoon, I decided, the moment had come. We began to pass narrow high-built bullock carts, and then the carriage entered the putrid streets of Telacamund, reeking of dung and incense. In front of almost every mud-house children with shiny red sores on their shaven heads scrambled and whined in the dust and excrement. A white-bearded Fakir, his nakedness daubed with filth, squatted motionless in contemplation. Native shopkeepers stood hopefully outside their tawdry shanty huts. Tamil women in faded saris with caste marks on their ebony foreheads stood aside to let us pass. The villagers stared at us apathetically with their dark eyes. Sometimes I fancied I could see a flash of resentment streak across a native's face, but when I looked again I could find nothing but dullness and indifference. Beside me, Anne sat so silent and so still that I wondered if she was even bothering to notice the filth and disease of this degenerate people or to smell the stench of dung and the sickly wafts of incense. I did not have to wonder for long. As the carriage left the last few derelict huts and moved into open country Anne spoke.

'I had no idea there was such poverty,' she said.

'You saw Madras,' I replied. 'It's worse down there.'

'But we don't live in Madras,' Anne said. 'We live here for a large part of the year. How can we exist in that huge house in such comfort while there's such poverty so close to us?'

I tried to control my irritation. 'My dear girl,' I said, 'the villagers were far poorer before we came to this place. There was no hospital. The English community has built them one. There were no welfare societies. Now we have half a dozen. They're better off for our presence, and they know it.'

'They're still wretchedly poor,' Anne persisted.

'So is the whole country,' I pointed out. 'But at least we're gradually improving their condition, and we're teaching them justice and the wisdom of good government. I don't know if you read our Viceroy's speech. I've memorised his very words. "Remember," he said to his English audience, "remember that the Almighty has placed your hand on the greatest of His ploughs. Remember—when your work is done—that you will rightly feel that somewhere among these millions you have left a little justice or happiness or prosperity, a sense of moral dignity, a spring of patriotism, a dawn of intellectual enlightenment, or a stirring of duty where it did not exist before—that is enough, that is the Englishman's justification in India." And I'm sure he's right.'

'I suppose so,' Anne said.

◆◆◆

Later that afternoon, I sent out the boy Sunil, our second syce, to escort Anne on her ride. Sunil is a Mission School lad, so he speaks a little English. As a groom he tends to be lazy and to skimp his work, but he is a good horseman. Anne rides well, I admit it. But it would, of course, be unthinkable to let her ride alone in this country which she hardly knows.

Apparently the little mare, Cara, behaved well for once, and Anne enjoyed the ride.

The following afternoon I drove down to the barracks with Anne in time for the three o'clock parade: I wanted her to see

Tom in his element. I confess a parade still has the power to thrill me. When we arrived, the whole Infantry Regiment was drawn up in line and at ease on the parade ground. The uniforms and regimental badges and buttons glittered in the sunshine. The Indian private soldiers looked very neat in their scarlet high-necked tunics with green sashes round their waists. Their short trousers were smartly creased, their puttees were evenly wound, and their chappals—as they call their sandals—were clean. Captain Rigg, who is a slim, lean, eager-looking man, was taking the parade. The Indian Regimental Sergeant-Major marched briskly towards him.

'All present and correct, sir,' he said in almost perfect English. 'Seven hundred on parade, sir.'

'Very good, Sergeant-Major,' Rigg answered.

At that moment Tom appeared on his horse, Jupiter. Poole, the Adjutant, was riding a few paces behind him. Tom looked magnificent. Rigg saluted Tom with his sword.

'Parade,' he shouted. 'Atten-shun!'

There was a click and a crash as the regiment moved; their bayonets gleamed in the sunshine. The straight rows of turbans were now motionless; the sooty-black faces beneath them were stern and resolute. Tom began to inspect the ranks. I glanced at Anne. She was watching the scene intently as if she were determined not to miss a single detail.

'This,' I thought to myself, 'this will teach the girl her position and the kind of man she has married.'

———◆◆◆———

As we drove home into the compound we had a glimpse of our two house-syces, Doshan and young Sunil, squatting over a plate of curry in a corner of the stableyard. I supposed that they had finished their afternoon's work and were hungry.

'Don't they eat with the rest of the servants?' Anne asked.

'No,' I replied, 'because they're from a different caste.'

'And that means they can't eat together?'

'Yes, indeed,' I answered. 'The Indians have amazingly severe restrictions about eating and cooking. Cooking is very important to them. A stranger's shadow falling on the cooking-pot—even the glance of a man of low caste—will ruin the whole meal. They'll just have to throw it all away.

'I don't understand,' Anne said.

'Nor do I,' was my answer. 'And nor do they, I very much suspect. Their customs are so complicated that even the books I've read and the experts I've listened to seem to get confused. But the rules of caste exist just the same.'

'How?' Anne asked. 'Try to explain.'

'I'll try,' I answered, secretly rather pleased that at last I was able to instruct her in some matter about which I had a slight knowledge. 'You see, we find the caste system a bit difficult to understand because we're used to class differences being vertical, as it were, from duke to chimney sweeper. *Their* differences can be vertical, but they're horizontal as well, so you can have different castes on more or less the same level. The word "caste" comes from the Portuguese word "casta", meaning breed, race or kind. One definition of it I've read is "a collection of families or groups of families bearing a common name, claiming a common descent from a mythical ancestor, following the same hereditary calling, and forming a single community". Members of a caste can't marry outside it.'

'But isn't it part of our duty here to abolish all those stupid prejudices?' Anne asked.

'Caste here has existed for thousands of years,' I told her. 'They believe that birth determines a man's caste for life. The Brahmins are at the top, then come the non-Brahmins, and lastly come the poor Untouchables. Incidentally, converts to Christianity come mostly from the lower castes. And there's an infinite number of sub-castes along the way. High caste Hindus are almost always lighter-skinned than those of a low caste. Even here in the south where, as you've seen, everyone seems to look prune-black, the words "dark" and "black" are terms of abuse. "Fair-skinned" is synonymous with "beautiful". It's a fetish, like their fear of being polluted. All Indian society is formed on these lines. We can't change it.'

'Isn't it our task to try to?' Anne enquired.

'What have we got to put in its place?' I asked her. 'New-

17

fangled ideas of equality? Our own system with all its pretence and incompetence? Let them be. Already they're changing slowly. An Indian will now tell you, "I'm a carpenter by caste, but I'm working as a mule-driver." Dancers represent one of the lowest and most polluted castes, yet they now earn so much money that I doubt if they care. Strictly speaking, the upper caste, the Brahmins, mustn't touch or be touched by a donkey or pig or dog, or a child old enough to eat solid food. He mustn't read a printed book while eating, nor a manuscript unless it's bound with silk and correctly pasted with tamarind. But I doubt, now, if every Brahmin sticks to the rules, or constantly considers his duties of studying, teaching, sacrificing, presenting alms, and receiving gifts. Give them time, and the Indians will change.'

I could see that Anne did not agree with me, so I concluded my little argument as briefly as I could.

'Our duty here, among others, is to educate the Indians and to show them another way of life,' I told her. 'But we mustn't undermine a system which, at present, is the very foundation of their society.'

'So Doshan and Sunil must still eat their rice in a corner of the stables?' Anne asked.

'Yes,' I answered crisply. 'That's just what they must do— so long as they remain in *our* employment. We have to try to see the problem of caste through Indian eyes. As it is, our behaviour is bad enough from their point of view. How can we expect a Brahmin, or any other Hindu, come to that, to hold us in esteem when we eat the flesh of the sacred cow— which to them is as bad an offence as eating human flesh? How can they admire us when they see us with servants of a despised caste—servants who are pariahs to their way of thinking? It's a difficult problem,' I concluded. 'It will take a long time to solve.'

3

Gradually I am beginning to learn my role.

When Tom is out, I sit with Margaret in the drawing-room and I read a book while she knits. Tom usually comes back for dinner. Each moment of each day is impressed on my memory. Last night, for instance, after my ride and a bath in the tub, there we were, the three of us, in the dining-room. I was sitting at the head of the table, with Margaret on my right and Tom facing me. Kumar, with his unpleasant smile, and fat Belur whom I rather like were standing in the background, ready to dart forward should one of us need anything. For a while there was silence. I could hear the grandfather clock ticking in the hall. Belur handed round a dish of stewed pears. Margaret leaned forward.

'I hope they've put in enough sugar for your taste,' she said to me.

I laughed. 'I'm very grateful,' I said. 'But to tell you the truth I'm not so very keen on sugar. Just because, on the way up here, I once said I thought some lemonade was sour, you and Tom have decided I like everything as sweet as syrup.'

Margaret stiffened. 'We want you to be happy,' she said.

'Thank you—both of you,' I said. 'You've been wonderfully kind to me.'

There was another silence. Margaret held up a spoon and turned to Kumar.

'This silver hasn't been properly cleaned,' she told him. 'See that it's better tomorrow.'

Kumar inclined his head. 'Yes, Memsahib,' he replied, and left the room.

As Tom and I were undressing that evening I approached him on a matter I'd been thinking over for some time.

'Tom,' I said, 'would you mind if every morning I taught in the English Mission School for three or four hours?'

Tom put his head round the door of his dressing-room.

'Teach in that horrid little school!' he exclaimed. 'You must be mad!'

'I've got almost nothing to do,' I told him. 'I'd like to make myself useful.'

'Useful? When you don't even know a word of Tamil?'

'Perhaps I could work in the hospital?'

Tom walked in from the dressing-room and put his arm round me. 'Listen, darling,' he said quietly. 'You are my wife. I'm jealous of you, and I'm jealous of your time. I want you to myself. What's more, when you've settled down here, there'll be entertaining and a hundred chores to do. Besides,' he added, 'I thought you used to amuse yourself by writing stories and poetry. If you've nothing to do in the morning, why not go back to your writing? Or have you given it up?'

'No,' I answered, 'I still write occasionally.'

'Then start again,' he said. 'I'm sure it will help to pass away a few hours.'

I said nothing. Later, in bed, he was unusually gentle with me. I try to love him at such moments. Perhaps one day I shall succeed.

My happiest moments occur in the late afternoon when I go out riding. Cara is a beautiful high-spirited and sensitive mare. We took to each other the first afternoon I rode her. Sunil, the groom—or syce as I must learn to call him—rides a chestnut gelding. He places himself discreetly some five yards behind me—as he has obviously been trained to do. I was delighted by the downs we galloped across and the forests through which we rode along a narrow track. I felt that my spirit had for a time at least been freed from the oppression of that gloomy house with its heavy dark mahogany furniture and its large high-ceilinged rooms. But after a mile or two of riding in silence I thought I ought to try to make some conversation with my escort.

Sunil is a young Tamil with a jet-black skin and a slightly surly expression when his face is in repose. Though his shoulders are broad, his waist is surprisingly slim, and he gives an impression of unusual vitality. Suddenly we moved out of the wood, and before us, shining like steel, was the lake. I turned round to Sunil.

'It's beautiful,' I said.

'Yes, Memsahib,' Sunil answered. His voice was hoarse with embarrassment.

'How old are you?' I asked gently.

Sunil lowered his long eye-lashes slowly.

'Eighteen,' he answered. 'Almost eighteen.'

'Do your parents live here in Telacamund?'

'Sorry?'

'Do your father and mother live here?'

Sunil waggled his head from side to side. It was surprising that he could perform a gesture which reminded me of a toy doll and still remain serious—graceful even.

'No, Memsahib. Father dead. Mother and my brother live beyond the sea.'

'Where?'

'In Ceylon.'

'Why did you come over here?'

'Because my people very poor. Because here I get good food and money.'

For once Sunil looked me direct in the face as our horses ambled along the track beside the lake. His eyes were large and very dark. I noticed how smooth the skin was on his face.

'One day, will you go back home?' I asked him.

'If the gods want it so,' Sunil answered.

At that moment we approached a small bungalow overlooking the lake. Leaning against the low wall which surrounded the property was a tall man, a European—at least I took him for a European because of his light-coloured skin, though he did not wear a solar topi which seems to be the badge of an Englishman in India. He was smoking a pipe. As we drew near to the wall abutting the track, the man took his pipe out of his mouth and waved to me cheerfully.

'Good evening,' he called out.

His accent was English. In a way his voice reminded me somehow of my father's.

'Good evening,' I answered.

'You don't know me,' he said smiling, 'so I hope you're not offended I should address you. But I know who you are. And my name's Rodney Meadows. This place is where I live. So if you're riding here some day and you feel a bit thirsty, please do stop and have some tea or a drink.'

'Thank you,' I replied. 'I'd like to.'

'Splendid,' Meadows said. 'I'll hope to see you. I'm generally about at this hour.'

'Thank you,' I repeated. 'Good evening.'

He waved again, and Sunil and I rode on.

We moved into a wood. Presently Sunil turned on to a track that led towards the place I must now learn to call home. The sun was slanting through the trees; monkeys were chattering in the branches above our heads. I began to wonder about Rodney Meadows. With his long creased face, clean-shaven and sunburned, he seemed quite attractive. His manner had been affable yet restrained; his soft voice had a kind of distinction. What could this apparently intelligent and amiable man be doing living alone—for so it seemed—in a decrepit bungalow at the end of the lake?

'Have you seen Mr Meadows before?' I asked Sunil.

'Yes, Memsahib,' Sunil answered. 'He has a plantation—tea-plantation—in the hills above the lake.'

Sunil then became silent. I felt that he was about to say more. I turned round to look at him, but he was staring at the ground ahead of him, and the faintly sullen expression had returned to his face.

Ahead of us we could now see Mickleden. Each time I saw the house with its neat balustrade running above the two rows of Georgian windows and its huge porch I was amazed that any building so typically English could ever have been built in the wilds of India. Only the wide verandahs and the elaborate carvings of the cornices showed any trace of the Orient. As we entered the compound we rode past a garishly constructed fountain which Tom said had not worked for over fifty years. Once again I became aware that the garden with its vivid clumps of shrubs and flowers offered the same odd contrast as did the house. Rose bushes and gardenias, lavender bushes and begonias and hollyhocks were mixed with exotic Indian plants. All of them were dominated by tall palm trees whose leaves rustled and clicked in the evening breeze.

We came into the stableyard. Sunil sprang from his saddle, crossed over to me, and cupped his hands together to help me dismount.

'Thank you, Sunil,' I said. I would have gone on to tell him how much I had enjoyed the ride, but I could see Margaret advancing towards us, and I knew she did not like me talking to the servants, so I said nothing to Sunil and moved away. I also had an instinct that Margaret would disapprove if she heard that a stranger had greeted me, so I decided not to mention my encounter with Mr Meadows outside his ramshackle bungalow with its high roof of hideous corrugated iron and its crumbling verandah.

4

I enjoy our Mess-nights up here in Telacamund. To start with, the air has been cool all day so that no one is exhausted or suffering from prickly heat. Secondly, even if one *does* get a bit tipsy, the cold night air will always sober one down.

I sit at the head of the table with Dawkin, my second-in-command, who is the Mess President, on my right. Poole, my Adjutant, with his ridiculously large moustache and beaky nose, sits on my left. The profusion of glasses on the table bears witness to the different wines we have already drunk. I look with an almost fatherly air at the fresh sunburned faces of the two rows of my officers, in their short jackets and cummerbunds and stiff collars with black silk ties. Decanters of port are now being passed round by six Tamil Mess-waiters, dressed in freshly starched uniforms, who glide neatly from place to place. There is a clatter of male voices. I glow with pleasure from the scene I am contemplating and from the wine I have drunk. For an instant I gaze up at the candles burning in the huge chandelier above the table. Suddenly, I think of Anne.

I think of Anne, and wonder what has gone wrong between us. But even as I wonder I begin to doubt if my concern is not due to my own imagination or to my own ignorance. Of course, I had had girls and women before my wedding night, but they were either professionals or eager amateurs. With Anne I knew it would be different. When she lay in bed that first night, staring up at me, I was certain that her nature was as ardent as I had guessed it would be. I knew that in the first moments

I was bound to hurt her; I hope that presently I would arouse a passion in her which would lessen the pain. But when it was all over I could see that the pain remained, and I was aware that there had been no ecstasy to overwhelm it.

The next morning, as I stood at the cheval-glass shaving myself, I could glance towards the bedroom and see Anne lying in bed, and I was appalled. I was appalled because the girl whom I had loved for so many years and whom I now loved more deeply than ever, looked hurt and bewildered, like a child who has been harmed by someone she trusts. I had hoped that in time—once the pain had gone—I could arouse desire in her. But even though she has now learned to simulate a kind of passion I can tell from various signs—the clenching of a hand or the tremor of her lips—I can tell the truth well enough. And I fear that I have failed. This failure has spread beyond our bedroom and now threatens to invade our whole relationship.

Certainly the life out here must in many ways seem strange to my young wife. For instance, Margaret tells me that Anne is too friendly with our servants. She tries to address them as if they were servants from our village at home in England. She cannot appreciate that an Indian bearer like Kumar or Belur is definitely embarrassed by the gentle tone of voice in which Anne addresses him. He is used to a clear command crisply given. But Margaret tells me that Anne refuses to learn this simple lesson. I feel that Anne has a fault—and I must admit this to myself—Anne is obstinate.

But at the moment I must try to forget about Anne; I must listen to Dawkin, my second-in-command, who is genially fuddled with drink and who is talking to Poole, my Adjutant, and to myself.

'Poor Hawkesbury,' Dawkin is saying. 'He was a good subaltern.'

Poole fingers his moustache as if to make certain that it is still there.

'He had a great career in front of him,' Poole says. 'Don't you agree, Colonel?'

I nod my head. Dawkin raises his glass solemnly.

'Let's drink to poor Hawkesbury,' Dawkin proposes. 'And to his wife and children.'

'Hawkesbury was a bachelor,' I feel obliged to point out. Dawkin is undeterred.

'Well, let's drink to the poor fellow just the same,' Dawkin says.

We raise our wine glasses and drink.

'We'd have had more dead from the heat of the plains if they hadn't moved us up here,' Poole states. By now he has re-assured himself that his moustache is in good order, and he has begun to crumble pellets of bread between his bony fingers.

'We lost eighteen men,' I remember sadly. 'That's quite a large number.'

Dawkin belches loudly and stares accusingly at Poole as if he were responsible.

'Even I was beginning to feel a bit seedy,' Dawkin admits. 'And I've been out here nearly twenty years. But brandy does the trick. Trust brandy every time.'

They go on talking. But my mind has turned back to Anne. It is a truism that we all have our faults. But Anne's particular fault of obstinacy is unfortunate out here in India. For instance, she is shocked by the poverty she sees, and she resents the Indian caste system. She refuses to appreciate that we are trying to do everything in our power to reduce the suffering in this vast land over which we have assumed complete responsibility. She cannot understand that it is impossible to break down overnight a system of caste which has lasted many thousands of years. We hold India by being in reality and in reputation a superior race. If this superiority did not exist we could not retain the country for one week. The more the natives of India are able to understand us, and the more we improve their capacity for understanding us, the firmer will our power become. Any idea of equal value for us and the Indian is plainly ridiculous. We must establish our rule over them by setting them a high example and by making them feel the worth of truth and honesty. I must persuade Anne to recognise these facts.

I will now make myself listen to the conversation on either side of me. I notice that Dawkin is gazing blearily down the table to make sure that each officer's glass has been filled with port.

'Personally, I prefer Simla,' Poole is saying. 'Don't you agree, Colonel?'

But I do not have to reply because suddenly Dawkin, as Mess President, stands up, and immediately all of us rise to our feet. For a moment there is silence. With a gesture of surprising dignity Dawkin raises his glass.

'Gentlemen,' he says. 'The Queen.'

At once, each one of us raises his glass, and in reverent tones from some thirty officers come the words: 'The Queen.'

'God bless her,' adds Dawkin.

We all drink and then sit down again. Dawkin reverts once more to the subject of Hawkesbury and brandy which seems very much on his mind tonight.

'Once I tried to get poor Hawkesbury to drink brandy,' he informs us. 'But he simply wouldn't touch the stuff.'

'He had a weak constitution,' says Poole. And I know that he is going to add—as he always does—the words, 'Don't you agree, Colonel?' I also know that I must not appear to be irritated. Sure enough he uses the words. But I smile at him. Then I survey my officers proudly.

'I don't think you'll find a weak constitution among our lot now,' I tell them. 'Ask the bearers to bring round more port.'

Presently—to Dawkin's delight—we begin to drink brandy. Once more my mind flicks back to Anne. I cannot help feeling that Anne is being a little ungrateful to me. I realise that I am by no means perfect—far from it. But the plain fact of the matter is that if I had not fallen in love with Anne when she was a very young girl, and if I had not married her, she might have been unable to have found herself a decent match, living as she did in the wilds of the country. After all, at least I have a good position and at least I have prospects. Yet Anne seems indifferent to such matters. There is a dreamy, impractical side to her nature which I must confess irritates me. For instance, consider her request to me to be allowed to teach in the mission school. What plan could be more ridiculous from every point of view? My dear sister Margaret—did any man ever have a more loyal friend?—runs the household so efficiently that any help from Anne would be redundant. But if Anne finds herself without anything to do she can visit the Telacamund library which is crammed full of books or she can stay at home and write her poems, and in the late afternoon she can go out riding on Cara. I have given her the little mare as a present. Surely she is leading a happier life out here than she would in the confines of a remote English farm? Yet, however much I argue with myself about Anne I still feel guilty about her in some odd way, and I cannot understand the reason why. After all, I have never ill-treated her. On the contrary. I try to be kind to her during every moment that we are together. Why then should I feel almost as guilty as if I had seduced the girl or raped her?

I know that I am beginning to get tipsy. But I can join in conversation with Dawkin and Poole while my mind still churns round in contemplation of Anne. Perhaps I am beginning to discover a possible reason for my guilt. There is a softness about Anne and a slimness about her body which reminds me of a young child. Her breasts are hardly formed; her skin bruises easily. Perhaps when I lie with her in bed I do indeed believe that I am seducing a child and, when the moment comes for me to take her, perhaps, as I thrust down into her narrow body, I do indeed think I am raping her. At this moment, surrounded by my officers, the idea disgusts me. But then I am not yet completely drunk.

Dinner is over. We are now standing in a cluster by the fireside in the ante-room, each with a glass of brandy in his hand. After a while we move back again into the dining-room. The long table has, by this time, been cleared. On the end of the table stand six empty wine bottles, unevenly spaced out. At the other end is a bench upon which, neatly poised, stands a young, fair-haired subaltern, Russell, who is married, alas, to a shrew of a wife. We have begun one of our favourite Mess-night games. In Russell's hand is a polo ball. With a swing of his arm he rolls the ball along the top of the table. It reaches the end and knocks down two bottles. There is mild applause from all of us who are gathered drunkenly around the bench. More bottles are placed in position. Dawkin now clambers up and takes young Russell's place. Amidst scattered cheers he is handed a polo ball and grips it tightly.

'I believe in the balloon approach,' Dawkin announces.

He throws the heavy ball high into the air. It crashes into the chandelier. Crystal pendants, broken glass and candles fall on to the table amidst wild laughter. Once again the table is cleaned up. Dawkin clambers down from the bench.

'Trust brandy to do the trick,' Poole says with a snigger.

Another young subaltern, Phillips, good-natured, plump, and sweating in his tight uniform, now steps up on to the bench. Expertly he rolls the ball along the table and knocks down four bottles. There are cries of 'Well done!' and some more applause. Now there are shouts of 'The Colonel! The Colonel!'

I smile. As I climb on to the bench my movements are a little unsteady. But my hand, when it grasps the polo ball, is firm. I prepare myself for the throw. The officers are so silent that I can hear the wall-clock ticking. I know instinctively that they are expecting me to score well and are hoping for my success. I look along the gleaming table. I fancy there is a slight bias to the left. Slowly I draw back my hand, then I send the ball springing. My throw is a lucky one. The ball knocks down all six bottles. I am moved by the loud cheering because I know that it is genuine and sincere. For an instant I gaze down, smiling at the faces of my officers. Then I decide that the time has come for me to return to Anne. Besides, I can remember that when I was a subaltern we always found the presence of our Colonel slightly restrictive on Mess-nights, however much we liked him.

'Now, gentlemen,' I say to them, 'if you'll excuse me, I'll take my leave.'

I climb down from the bench.

'But don't let me break up the party,' I add as I move towards the door which is opened by young Phillips whose hair has now fallen dankly over his forehead. There are cries of, 'Good-night, sir,' from junior officers, and 'Good-night, Colonel,' from the senior officers.

I stand in the porch for a moment and peer out into the darkness for my head syce. From inside I hear the crash of glasses, the splintering of wood, and then hilarious laughter. Two officers are talking in the ante-room. I cannot tell who they are because their voices are so blurred.

'Well, what did you do with the fellow?' one of them asks.

'Dismissed the whole charge,' the other officer replies. 'And let the man go.'

I am definitely feeling drunk. I shout for my syce.

'Doshan!' I bellow. 'Where are you?'

At that instant, Doshan appears leading my horse, Jupiter, a black stallion. I grin at Doshan.

'Asleep as usual I suppose,' I say to him. Doshan's wizened face creases like leather as he smiles.

'No, Colonel Sahib,' he answers.

I am glad that I am not so drunk that he has to help me to mount. I spring into the saddle. I press my legs against the horse's sides. 'Good-night, Doshan,' I call out.

Soon I am galloping fast along the moonlit track that leads up to Mickleden. The air is splendidly fresh. I feel confident and elated. I don't have to spur Jupiter. He knows he is heading for home. He is as exhilarated as I am. The night-watchman opens the gate of the compound. A sleepy Tamil boy lets me into the house which is partly in darkness, for Margaret and Anne have gone to bed some hours ago. I stagger up the stairs. Now that I am indoors again, my drunkenness returns. I open the bedroom door and lock it behind me as I always do nowadays. The embers of the fire glow beneath the marble mantelpiece. A paraffin lamp, turned low, is still burning. Anne is lying in bed, reading a book, as I lurch in. Anne closes her book and puts it on the bedside table.

'Still awake?' I ask. I can hear that my voice is slurred.

'I can't sleep,' Anne explains.

I cross over to her and begin to stroke her hair. 'My little darling,' I mutter.

Anne does not move. I slide my hand beneath her nightdress and begin to fondle her breasts. I bend down and kiss her on the mouth while my other hand moves under the bedclothes. Anne slips away from my embrace. I begin to strip off my clothes. Anne stares at me. In my silly drunkenness I hope she is admiring my figure. I have always tried to keep myself fit—even though I sometimes do drink heavily.

'I can't,' Anne blurts out suddenly.

'You can't?' I repeat stupidly. 'Can't what?'

'You must sleep in the dressing-room. Because I don't . . .' Anne begins, then she stops herself as if she were afraid of what she had been about to say. 'Please, Tom,' she continues. 'Just for tonight.'

'What were you going to say?' I ask her.

'It doesn't matter,' Anne answers quietly.

For some reason, her reticence enrages me. I stride over to her.

'What were you going to say?' I repeat.

Anne is silent. I grasp her shoulders.

'You're hurting me,' Anne says.

'Tell me,' I now insist.

I clutch her arm. Anne gives a gasp of pain.

'Tell me,' I shout at her.

'Then let go,' Anne cries out.

I move away from her bed. For a moment there is silence.

'I was going to say,' Anne begins, 'I was going to say, Tom, please leave me alone—just for tonight.'

'No!' I cry. Suddenly I wonder. 'You've not got . . .' I begin.

Anne shakes her head wearily. 'No,' she murmurs. 'It's not that. But let me alone—for tonight.'

I glare at her in confusion. I feel angry and frustrated. Where is the eager, impetuous young girl I married?

'Please,' Anne continues almost incoherently. 'Please go to the dressing-room. You can sleep on the bed in there.'

I gaze at her with incomprehension.

'You don't even want me to lie with you?' I ask.

I can see that in a moment Anne will break down and cry.

'I'm sorry,' Anne whispers. 'Please forgive me, Tom. It's only for tonight, I promise you.'

'You've already said that once before,' I point out.

Tears are now forming around Anne's eyelids. 'Tom,' she mutters, 'I'm sorry.'

Awareness of my marital rights, established by law, surge through my drunken mind.

'You're my wife,' I begin. Then I realise how hopeless it is to try and explain my position in words. Once again, I move towards the bed. I stand close to her. I can see her staring at my nakedness. The idea comes into my mind that if I were now to get into the bed and force her to submit to me, if I were to take her violently and cruelly, then at last I might arouse some passion in her. But as I glower down at her I see the fear in her eyes. For an instant I hesitate. Part of me is excited by her fear, and this part wishes to inflict pain into her so that she will moan as she submits. Another part of me—the part that loves her—tells me that for tonight at least I must leave her alone. So I turn away from her. I stumble across to my dressing-room. I close the door behind me.

<hr/>

The following morning I must admit I awoke feeling sick. But as soon as I got out of bed and had stood by the window, taking in long breaths of the delicious cool morning air, I felt better. I was glad that Anne was still asleep when I left the house.

After parade that morning I rode back home. When I came into the room Margaret was sitting alone, sewing, in the high-backed chair.

'How are things at the barracks?' Margaret asked me.

'We never have much trouble up here,' I told her. 'It's down in the heat that everything goes wrong, as you well know.'

Kumar came in carrying a burrapeg of whisky for me on a large tray. 'Is lunch ready?' I asked Margaret.

'When you are,' Margaret answered.

I took a gulp of my drink. I had already had a quick chotapeg down in the Mess. But I needed drink that morning.

'Where's Anne?' I enquired.

Margaret's mouth slid in a nervous tic and then tightened.

'In her sitting-room,' Margaret answered.

I gaped at her. 'Where?' I asked.

'It was her idea,' Margaret explained apologetically. 'Anne said she wanted a room where she could be alone to do her writing. So we took down some old furniture from the attic and put it in that empty room facing the stableyard.'

I am always annoyed when anyone moves my furniture about without my consent. I took another gulp of my drink.

'Why wasn't I told?' I demanded.

Margaret could see that I was angry. She dropped her sewing. Her hands began to flutter like moths.

'Because you weren't here,' she explained. 'The great move only happened this morning. You're annoyed, but what was I to do?'

She looked up at me. Her nervous tic had started once again. 'Tom, don't be angry with me,' she said.

Immediately I could feel the rage draining out of me as I remembered how devoted my darling Margaret had always been. I crossed the room and went over to the chair and put my arms around her.

'I'm not angry,' I said. 'I'm just surprised.' I finished my drink. 'I think I should go and inspect,' I announced.

As I left the room, Margaret sighed, and I do not know why. Was it because I had been cross with her, or was it a sigh of recollection of those days when the two of us had lived alone together here at Mickleden in such peace and satisfaction?

The small room which Anne had chosen was on the ground floor of the house, overlooking the yard. When I came in, my first impression was that the odd pieces of furniture that had been taken from the attic had been placed attractively. Bright flowers in jars stood on each table. Anne was sitting at a desk which had been placed by the window. She was hurriedly sliding a sheet of paper into the drawer of the desk as I came in. She snatched up a book and pretended to read. I was amused that she should be so furtive about the poetry she wrote. When I closed the door behind me, Anne put down the book and smiled up at me. I looked around, inspecting it all.

'You've arranged the furniture better than I'd have thought possible,' I said.

'I like the shape of the room,' Anne replied.

For a moment there was silence. Rain was streaming down the window-panes, and the yard was turning to mud.

'I've got the afternoon free,' I said. 'I thought we might stay in and play cards. Would you like that?'

'Yes,' Anne answered. 'Yes, I would.'

———◆◆◆———

I told Kumar to place the card-table in Anne's new sitting-room. That afternoon, Anne and I sat in front of the fire playing bezique. Anne was extremely quiet. Suddenly I felt that I could endure the strain between us no longer. I put down my cards. I looked up at her.

'I'm sorry,' I said. 'About last night, I mean.'

'You needn't be,' Anne answered. 'I expect it was my fault in a way.'

Once again there was silence. I leaned forward and touched her hand. 'Anne,' I said, 'you do know I love you?'

Anne glanced up at me, then smiled rather sadly.

'Yes,' she replied. 'Yes, I know.'

'Perhaps in time,' I began.

Anne nodded her head. 'I'm sure,' she said. 'Of course I'm sure.'

With that I had to be content. I began to deal the cards.

5

The evenings I have to spend with Margaret are so long that I can recall each detail without any effort. The furniture in the drawing-room which is a strange mixture of English tables and sofas of various periods has been gathered together haphazardly. The cretonnes do not match, and the Chippendale looking-glass is spotted with mildew. There are brass-topped coffee-tables and elephant-tusks on either side of the chimney-piece beneath which a few logs are burning. Beyond the fender is a panther-skin rug. A gaudy Indian carpet, bought in Madras, covers the rest of the floor. Margaret, aloof and stern-faced, is sewing by the light of a single oil lamp; I am reading by the light of the other lamp. Moths, beetles and flies flutter around the lamp-shades and hurl themselves at the hot glass of the chimneys. The fire crackles. Margaret puts down her sewing and looks towards me.

'Would you like a glass of wine or some tea?' Margaret asks.

'Neither, thank you, Margaret,' I reply.

Again there is silence. A log of wood falls from the fire-basket on to the grate, and I replace it. This at least is an event for my evening.

'What's that book you're reading?' Margaret enquires.

'Some poems by Byron,' I answer.

Margaret glances up at me disapprovingly and then looks down at her sewing. 'I prefer Lord Tennyson,' she announces. 'A great favourite of our dear Queen.' Her hands are still for a moment. 'Do you paint?' she enquires suddenly.

'No,' I reply. 'Why do you ask?'

'You seem the artistic type,' Margaret says. 'I thought you might try your ability at a water-colour. It would give you something to while away the time.'

I am fond of Margaret. Or at least I try to like her because she is Tom's sister. But her remarks are quite unpredictable. I never quite know what lies behind each sentence she speaks.

'Don't worry,' I say. 'I'm perfectly happy reading poetry.'

Margaret looks at the clock on the mantelpiece. She rises from her chair.

'I think it's time to go to bed,' she tells me.

I get up and follow Margaret to the door. Our evening together is at an end.

———◆◆◆———

It is true that I haven't much to entertain me when Tom is down at the barracks. But at least I have my afternoon ride. And gradually Sunil, the young syce, is becoming less shy in my presence. Yesterday he even made a remark all on his own. We had been galloping along a track through the wood. My mare, Cara, was moving beautifully. Sunil was following close behind. Presently I reined in and we stopped in a clearing. Sunil on his chestnut gelding came up beside me.

'Memsahib ride well,' he blurted out.

I smiled at him. 'Thank you, Sunil,' I replied. 'So do you.'

Sunil looked down at his hands. He was wearing cotton gloves. I could see that he was growing shy again.

'Memsahib like to drink the air,' he said nervously.

'Drink what?' I asked.

Sunil smiled. I have noticed that he is always pleased when he knows something about which I am ignorant. In fact I often pretend ignorance to make him happy. Sunil now breathed in deeply, expanding his chest and then exhaling the air again.

'We say "drink the air" when we breathe much,' Sunil explained. 'You like?'

'Yes,' I answered. 'Yes, I do.' I smiled at him. Once again I was aware of the smoothness of his ebony-coloured skin.

'Speaking of drink,' I said, 'I'm thirsty. Did you fill my water-flask?'

'Yes,' Sunil answered.

Our horses were still side by side. I took up my flask, pulled off its cup and poured out some water. Without thinking I handed it first to Sunil. For a moment he hesitated. The sullen expression had returned to his face. Then he stretched out one of his hands, still encased in a cotton glove. He leaned forward in his saddle and took the cup and drank a little water. He seemed so worried by this action that I felt some gesture of reassurance was necessary. Almost without thinking I raised my hand and for a moment I gently touched the skin of his cheek. Sunil flinched as if he had been struck.

'What is it, Sunil?' I asked.

'For my sins,' he began, and then stopped. I remembered that he had been taught English in the mission school, and sometimes odd phrases from some religious teaching would enter into his colloquial speech. 'For my sins,' Sunil continued, stammering a little in his confusion, 'for my sins, I am not of your caste. That is why I must wear gloves. So I do not touch you.'

'But, Sunil,' I said, 'you were at a Christian mission school. You can't believe that people should be divided by caste?'

Sunil glanced at me. I noticed his long curling eye-lashes. There were a few drops of sweat on his forehead.

'What else can I believe?' Sunil demanded. 'When every Hindu I meet tells me so.'

'I think you're too intelligent and too kind to believe in such a harsh creed,' I said.

Sunil turned in the saddle and stared at me. His dark eyes seemed to grow wide in a look of desperate entreaty.

'Then will you help me?' Sunil asked. 'They taught me very little at the mission school. Will you help me to learn? Will you find me books, so I can be less ignorant? So I can better myself?'

For a second I hesitated because I knew that if Tom found out, he would be angry with me. But as I contemplated the expression on Sunil's face, I felt that I could not refuse his harmless request.

'Yes, Sunil,' I answered. 'I will.'

⸻

We were now approaching the tumbledown bungalow at the end of the lake, and I saw Rodney Meadows, the planter who had previously greeted me. He was talking to a Tamil boy mending the fence at the end of the compound. As we approached he waved to us once again and walked down the hillside on to the track.

'Hasn't it been a wonderful afternoon?' he said, smiling up at me. 'Can I persuade you to stop for a drink on the verandah?'

Then as he saw me hesitate, he added, 'And I'm sure that my bearer will be only too delighted to offer your syce any drink he likes.'

His long face was wrinkled in a smile. There was something pleasing about his quiet voice. Perhaps Tom would disapprove if he heard about it, but I saw no reason why I should not accept the invitation.

'Thank you very much,' I replied.

⸻

Presently I was drinking a glass of wine on his verandah. Sunil had disappeared into the servants' quarters with a Tamil bearer. I had set out on the ride earlier than usual so I had plenty of time. I soon felt happily at ease with Rodney Meadows because he seemed so much at ease with himself.

'How long have you been out here?' I asked him.

'In Telacamund or in India?'

'In India.'

He sipped his brandy. 'Fifteen years,' he replied.

He must have noticed my look of surprise, for he added, 'I began my existence here in the Army.' He paused. His grey eyes watched me in amusement. 'You're now wondering why I'm not a Colonel like your husband,' he laughed.

'I am,' I answered. 'But, incidentally, do tell me how you knew that I was married to Tom when I first rode past here?'

'Answer number one,' he began. 'Because out here in our small community everyone knows *almost* everything about everyone else. Answer number two: I left the Army because I hated it.'

'Why?' I asked.

For a while he was silent. His face had suddenly grown sad. 'You're married to a Colonel, so you practically belong to your husband's way of life,' he said. 'I don't want to say anything to prejudice you against the Army.'

'Please don't worry,' I replied. 'I'm not a child.'

He laughed, and for a moment the sadness disappeared from his face. 'Sometimes you *look* like a child,' he said. 'But I suppose I'd best get my story quickly over and done with. I'm afraid it's an unhappy and unpleasant one. There was a man in my troop who was on a charge for getting drunk and insulting an officer. This trooper of mine was very ugly and very stupid. But for some reason I was fond of him. I did my best for him at the court-martial, but he was sentenced to be flogged. The sentence was carried out savagely. A week later the man died in hospital. The whole business disgusted me. But it was more than that. I felt I just didn't *belong* to my regiment—or to any other regiment come to that. I was a misfit. So I thought the matter over for a while, and then I sent in my papers.'

Rodney Meadows finished his glass of brandy and poured himself another. I had been disgusted and appalled by his story. But some of the books I had read about India made me appreciate he was telling the truth.

'But for various reasons I didn't want to leave India,' he concluded. 'Luckily I had a bit of money. So eventually I bought this ramshackle place with its tea-plantation.'

'Are you glad you decided to stay in India?' I asked him.

He looked down at his glass. 'I think so,' he answered. 'What about yourself? Are you happy out here?'

'Yes,' I replied quickly. 'I love Telacamund.'

There was a brief silence.

'I suppose you're going to the Rajah's garden-party to-morrow?' he asked.

'I believe so,' I answered. 'It will be the first time that I've met him. Shall I see you there?'

'Great heavens no!' Rodney Meadows exclaimed.

His tone was so violent that I glanced at him in surprise. 'Why not?' I asked.

'Even if they did invite me—which is most unlikely—I wouldn't go,' he said. 'It's the Resident and his associates who send out the list of the suitable people to invite, at the Rajah's request, needless to say. And I don't like the Resident, and I don't like his officials. I hate and despise almost every single one of them.'

He took a gulp of his drink. 'And shall I tell you why?' he demanded with a wave of his hand. 'Because they're almost all of them hypocrites, and they belong to one of the greatest hypocritical concepts the world has ever known. As you certainly know, Britain has the largest Empire in the history of the world. It controls a quarter of the earth and a quarter of its population. And why has our country assumed this responsibility? Because we have managed to persuade ourselves to believe that we were appointed by God to rule over all these hordes of natives. We have become convinced that we are a superior race. But in truth there's only one principle we hold—which is basic to all others—that is, in one word, profit. The deepest passion of our Empire is to be rich. Every item we need from rice to zinc flows effortlessly into our pockets. So that we are now the richest and most powerful country in the world.'

He paused and poured some wine into my glass although it was still half full.

'But there's another side to the coin,' he continued. 'Let me give you some examples. For instance, two English planters wanted to get a confession from a young native Indian syce they had employed in Calcutta. They were convinced he had stolen some money. Accordingly they stripped the boy naked and tied him up to a tree, and they took turns in flogging him all afternoon. He died that evening. The two of them had, in effect, murdered the boy, so they carried off his body and buried it.

Later their crime was discovered. They were duly charged with murder. But other planter friends of theirs subscribed one thousand pounds for their defence, and the two planters were sentenced to only three years' imprisonment. Even that sentence was considered a harsh one. Here's another example. An English official in Delhi lost his temper with his coachman. He pulled the Indian down into the road and kicked him to death. In court the official was fined thirty rupees—the equivalent of a couple of pounds. I'm only speaking about cases that have come into court. But brutality of a most horrible kind flourishes. And there's almost always a local doctor who will sign a death certificate without question. When they come out here from England, soldiers are officially told to be careful, when they beat natives, not to touch their faces, because the bruises will show. And all this cruelty exists in all parts of the Empire under the hypocritical façade of our blessed Imperial Rule. And do you suppose for an instant that we ever intend to leave India? Never. So long as half-starved natives can be whipped and tortured to work, so long as we share some of the loot with their Rajahs and overseers, so long as an essentially decent man, like your husband, can sincerely persuade himself that his regiment is here for the general benefit of the Indian culture and way of life, then England will stay in India until the crack of doom.'

He was getting slightly drunk. I put down my glass and rose from my chair.

'Now I've offended you,' he muttered.

'Yes,' I answered. 'You've upset me very much. But perhaps these things have to be said. Meanwhile, I need time to think over what you have told me. I want to measure it against the code of behaviour which Tom believes in and for which he would gladly die. I'm still confused in my own mind. So, if you will excuse me, I'll leave now.'

He nodded his head. In silence he escorted me to the gate of the compound where Sunil was waiting with our two horses.

On the way home I began trying to improve Sunil's English. I had already determined to get him some books from the library. I had to force myself to concentrate on the words I was teaching him, for I had been greatly disturbed by what Sunil had said to me about caste, and I had been upset by my meeting with Rodney Meadows.

———◆◆◆———

As I watched the light filtering into our bedroom the following morning, and as I watched Tom's dark head of hair on the pillow beside me, a line of poetry came into my mind. Soon I believed I had a vague idea for a sonnet. That morning I made an excuse so that I did not have to accompany Margaret on her shopping expedition. I wandered into my sitting-room and sat down at my desk. At first I could only think of one line. But then it all became clear. I could see a young girl living in rather similar circumstances to myself. I was fascinated by the situation in which this girl had been placed by fortune. I worked on the sonnet all morning. Then I wrote down the final draft. When I had finished it, I tore up the sheets of paper on which I had scribbled various lines. I put my completed sonnet away in my desk drawer. I was locking the drawer when Margaret came in to tell me that lunch was ready.

Blow winds about the house, you cannot shake me,
    However blustering or strong you blow!
March military feet, you will not wake me
    However loud you trample to and fro!
Go, grim command rapped out, you cannot make me
    Do what I would not. This alone I know,
An inward restlessness will not forsake me,
    A restlessness that does not let me go.

Day after day I feel my body tingling.
    Night after night I hope that, far or near,

Some being waits whose soul with mine commingling
  Will fill the emptiness I suffer here.
I yearn for love, deep, tender, trusting, steady,
Oh unknown lover, now my heart is ready.

———————◆◆◆◆———————

Tom, in his full-dress uniform, and Margaret, in a mauve gown
were already in the hall when I came down the stairs that
afternoon, wearing a pale-blue muslin dress which Margaret
had helped me choose for my trousseau.

'We'll be late,' Tom said.

'I don't suppose the Rajah will behead us,' Margaret replied.

She seemed in an unusually good humour, and I noticed she
had dabbed a little powder on her face.

'You look really pretty,' she told me.

'That's true enough,' Tom added.

'Thank you,' I said. 'Bless you both. I've done my best for
the occasion.'

Doshan, the head syce, drove us in the carriage up the hillside.
Presently we turned into the long grass-lined avenue of rhodo-
dendrons and cannas which led to the Rajah's palace. As we
approached the impressive portico we could see other carriages
lined up the drive. The palace was a fantastic building, half
oriental and half English, with tall Corinthian columns flanking
the central section and huge pink domes of crumbling stucco on
either side.

Tom helped Margaret and me from the carriage. Together
the three of us walked up the marble steps and passed between
two rows of the Rajah's Guard of Honour drawn up beneath
the portico, their dark skins shining above their scarlet tunics.
As we advanced we were greeted by the Rajah's Chamberlain,
an elderly grey-haired Indian who was both affable and elegant.
We passed through a vast hall in which hung elaborate chan-
deliers. Each corner was festooned with banners. A thick
turquoise-blue carpet seemed to stretch the length of the
palace. As we moved through suite after suite of rooms, I

became so amazed that I could no longer take in the whole profusion of furniture. I was vaguely aware of an abundance of gilt chairs and crimson divans and of a multitude of garish vases and beautifully carved ivory figures.

On the wide expanse of the lawn on the far side of the palace were assembled the officers of Tom's regiment with their wives and a few civilian officials including the Resident, Gerald Maxwell, who Tom said always looked as if he had swallowed a ramrod. He was accompanied by his wife, a tall domineering lady with a hawk-nose and a mouth as straight as the slit of a letter-box. The Rajah was talking to Frank Russell's wife, Marjorie. She was a pretty dark-haired girl, buxom and attractive with a provocative manner. I had heard that the Rajah had the reputation of being indiscreetly fond of young English girls, and now, as he talked with Marjorie, I could sense that he was exerting his charm. The Rajah was a handsome man, slim and neatly built, with a lean sharply pointed face which gave him a slightly wolfish appearance until he smiled. He was dressed in a dark-blue silk tunic with large ruby buttons, surrounded by pearls, and tight-fitting silk trousers. The famous Mysore diamond which had belonged to his family for over a thousand years blazed in his orange-coloured turban. As soon as the Rajah saw Tom he bowed to Marjorie Russell and moved forward to greet us. He gave Margaret a polite nod of his head and then turned to Tom. At that moment, as Tom saluted him, I had the feeling that I was watching two kings meet. The Rajah joined the tips of his fingers together in oriental greeting.

'I'm so glad you could come,' he murmured. He spoke almost perfect English.

Tom smiled at him, then inclined his head towards me.

'This is my wife,' Tom announced.

I walked towards the Rajah and curtsied. As he took my hand his eyes seemed to be searching my face.

'It is an honour and a pleasure to meet you,' he said.

Suddenly the Rajah turned back to Tom and smiled at him politely. 'By the way, my dear Colonel, I almost forgot,' he said. 'I can't let you have manœuvres beside the lake. I'm afraid I've arranged for a shikar ending in a leopard hunt.'

Tom nodded his head stiffly. 'Then I'll make different arrangements,' he answered.

'Thank you,' the Rajah replied, and turned once more to me as a bearer appeared with a tray of drinks. With an odd little swoop of his hand the Rajah picked up a glass of champagne from the tray, handed it to me, and then took a glass for himself. The bearer moved towards Tom and Margaret.

'It is a long time since I saw your country so perfectly represented on these lawns,' the Rajah told me.

'How long were you in England?' I asked him.

'I was three years at Oxford,' the Rajah answered.

'Did you enjoy them, sir?' I asked.

'Please don't call me "sir", or "highness",' the Rajah said, 'for you and I meet as equals.'

I smiled. 'But did you enjoy Oxford?'

'No,' he answered. 'Not very much.'

'May I ask the reason?'

'You may,' the Rajah replied. 'You may ask anything you please—though I don't promise I will always answer you. But this question I *can* answer. I was not happy there because in many ways I was made aware that my skin was not white.'

The Rajah smiled grimly as he looked round at Tom's officers. 'Nor even red or sunburned,' he added. 'But what was worse was that I didn't even play cricket. However, some of your people were quite friendly to me. In fact, for a moment they would forget my colour and treat me as a friend. But the next moment, if by mistake I displeased them, they would turn on me and I would be called a dirty nigger.'

'I'm sorry,' I said quietly. I was embarrassed, but I was determined not to show it. 'I'm afraid cruelty exists in every country and in every kingdom. I daresay there are as many taboos here in Telacamund as in Oxford.'

'You mean our system of caste?' he asked.

'Yes,' I answered. 'And other forms of cruelty. A man being lashed to death for instance.'

The Rajah was gazing at me sadly.

'But here in my State,' he said, 'we do not even pretend to be emancipated as all you English do. However, I enjoyed the holidays in England when I could ride around alone in your beautiful countryside.'

As he spoke, I noticed that a few of the Indian and European guests were glancing towards the two of us as we stood talking on the lawn. I now also observed a strange-looking Indian, rather shabbily dressed in European clothes, who was loitering behind the Rajah. His head was bald on top. But thick locks of greasy hair fell down on to his neck which was very thin. There was something predatory about the expression of his narrow emaciated face. At last the man managed to get into the line of the Rajah's vision. He moved forward quickly and salaamed. The Rajah introduced him curtly.

'May I present Ashur, my cousin and my secretary?' he asked me in a voice cold with formality.

Ashur salaamed to me respectfully.

'Tell the bearer to bring some champagne to the Colonel,' the Rajah said to him briskly. 'I see his glass is empty.'

Ashur inclined his head and moved away.

'Yes, I love your countryside,' the Rajah continued. 'And, if I may say so, you bring with you all the grace and fragrance of it. But now you must excuse me, for I must "circulate", as you put it, among my guests. Will you do me the honour of coming to tea with me? My wife is indisposed today, but if you and your husband will do me the honour of coming to tea on Thursday she will be there.' The Rajah smiled once more, and immediately his face became transformed, and he looked a pleasant, though perhaps mischievous, young man. 'So it will all be quite proper,' he added. 'Even if your husband can't accompany you, will you and your husband's sister come?'

'I'd love to,' I answered. 'I don't know about Tom and Margaret.'

Once again the Rajah joined the tips of his fingers together. As his hands parted the jewels he was wearing flashed and shimmered in the sun. He turned round and moved towards a group of his guests. As soon as the Rajah had left, Marjorie Russell came up to me. Her face was shining and her hat was a trifle lopsided. Eagerly she snatched a glass of champagne from a bearer who was passing by.

'Well!' she exclaimed. '*There* was a success if ever I saw one!'

'He was only being polite to me,' I protested.

Marjorie laughed. 'My dear, his eyes were positively devouring you,' she said.

'Nonsense,' I replied. 'He just happens to have rather luminous eyes.'

'Luminous!' Marjorie said with a titter. 'What quaint words you do use! But then I forget. You're an intellectual. I mean, you read poetry and all that.'

Olivia Maxwell, the wife of the Resident, now loomed towards us.

'I was just congratulating Anne on her success with the Rajah,' Marjorie told her.

For some reason I felt obliged to apologise. 'I was a new face,' I explained. 'That's all.'

Marjorie gave another titter. 'We can leave that to your husband to decide,' she said.

Olivia Maxwell's letter-box mouth stretched into a smile as it generally did when anyone mentioned the Rajah. As the wife of the Resident she always assumed a protective, almost motherly attitude towards the Rajah. Sometimes—to hear her speak—you would think she owned him.

'Dear Nikki!' she exclaimed. 'He's just a boy at heart. He can't resist flirting with every woman he meets. I don't mind telling you he makes my husband quite jealous. In fact, I'm beginning to think he rather prefers mature women,' she continued, patting her abundant grey hair into position and then adjusting the hang of her skirt.

'He certainly seems at his happiest in your company,' Marjorie told her, sliding down her empty glass of champagne on to a bearer's tray and seizing another.

'Nikki and I are old friends,' Olivia Maxwell said, shifting her massive shoulders coyly. 'Many is the political row I've managed to quell. A little flattery here and a little tact there. You know, it's not really as difficult as you might think.' She smiled at us pleasantly. 'But now you'll have to forgive me,' she announced. 'I simply must go and talk to the vicar's wife. She may be dowdy, but she's awfully sweet to the poor man when he gets drunk.'

Olivia Maxwell paused and stared at Marjorie's hat which was by now definitely askew.

'I do wish that every member of our community, out here in Telacamund, would learn the lesson of self-control—if not of abstinence,' she added, accentuating each syllable as if she were in a lecture-hall. 'After all, each one of us should remember that he—or she—is here to set an example to the natives.'

With this remark she moved off, and soon Marjorie drifted away in the opposite direction. Tom came up to me. I could see that he was displeased.

'Try to avoid him for the rest of the afternoon,' he said quietly.

'Try to avoid whom?' I asked. 'You can't mean the Rajah?'

Tom made a little grimace. 'Everyone was looking at the two of you,' he told me.

'Let them,' I replied. 'It was all perfectly innocent, I assure you.'

'That wasn't how it looked,' Tom answered.

'Tom,' I began, 'you can't really think . . .'

'I'm not sure,' he interrupted. 'The man has quite a reputation.'

I smiled at Tom. It gave me a strange pleasure to know that he was jealous.

'Well, you *should* be sure,' I informed him. 'You don't need to worry. And I have to confess to you that I've accepted his invitation for the three of us to have tea with him and his wife on Thursday.'

'Why?' Tom asked.

'Because we were invited,' I explained.

'I can't possibly get away from the barracks, and you could have made an excuse,' Tom said.

'I didn't want to refuse,' I answered. 'I like him. He amuses me.'

Though I could see that Tom was annoyed with me, he managed to smile.

'All right,' he said. 'But now you'd better go and talk to the Judge's wife. Perhaps she'll amuse you too.'

6

I knew that when she was in her sitting-room Anne spent part of her time writing, and I found it curious that she had never shown either Tom or me anything she had written. My experience of those who write or paint is that they are only too willing to show their latest effusion to any relative or friend who can be persuaded to examine it. Why then was Anne so secretive about her work? Why had I once come into her room to discover her locking up the drawer of her desk?

Before I made the decision to go into her sitting-room and make an exploration, I searched my heart. I wanted to make certain that my motives were altruistic. Personally I had no interest at all in Anne's efforts as a writer. But I had a firm instinct which told me that the solution to Anne's relationship with Tom lay in whatever she had put down on paper. And I was worried about them both for, of course, I was aware that, so far, the marriage had not been a success. Our mother had died in giving birth to Tom when I was only five years old. Though there was a nurse and a nursemaid to look after him, it was I who took the responsibility for his welfare. For over fifty years I have been Tom's closest friend and ally, so my intuition about him is unusually perceptive. I know when he is worried or unhappy. These last weeks he has been both. Eventually, after a week of doubt, my concern for Tom's happiness outweighed my scruples. I decided to inspect Anne's study.

I waited until Anne had gone out for her afternoon ride with Sunil. Then I entered the room. Fortunately the stableyard was empty, so no one could observe my search. On top of the desk were a dozen sheets of unused writing-paper. I then discovered that several sheets of paper had been burned in the fireplace. The drawer of the desk was locked. I doubted if Anne would have taken the key out of the room. I looked around. I opened a lacquer pencil-box, but it was empty. Then I noticed a Benares vase on the mantelpiece. I shook it, and there was a rattling sound. I held it up-side-down. A key fell out. I put the key into the lock of the desk and turned it. The drawer opened. On top was a single sheet of paper with writing on it. I put on my spectacles, took out the sheet and began to read. It was a poem written in what I believe is known as sonnet-form. I looked into the stableyard. There was still no one about. I read the poem.

I am aware that when a young girl writes poetry she allows her day-dreams to enter her consciousness. But this poem went beyond the usual romantic yearnings of a young girl. Within the lines I found a distinct resentment of Tom's authority and a definitely sensual longing to have a lover. For a while I was so angry that I could not move. The lines blurred. I stood staring down at the sheet of paper trembling in my hands. Then I regained control over myself. I put the poem back in the desk; I locked the drawer, and I dropped the key into the Benares vase. I went back into the drawing-room.

Two hours later I was sitting in an armchair, pencil in hand, with a ledger-book on my lap, doing the household accounts, when Tom came in.

'I thought you were dining tonight in Mess,' I said.

'I changed my mind,' Tom replied. 'Where's Anne?'

'Upstairs,' I answered. 'The ayah's preparing a bath for her, after her evening ride.'

I saw that the glass of whisky in Tom's hand looked suspiciously dark.

'Aren't you drinking rather a lot these days?' I enquired.

'I hadn't noticed it,' Tom answered.

I put down the ledger-book. I spoke very quietly. 'Is she making you unhappy?' I asked.

'No,' Tom replied. 'Is there any reason why she should?'

'Yes.'

'What is the reason?' Tom asked. He was glaring at me.

Until that moment I had not made up my mind how far I would go in warning him about Anne. I was now convinced I must tell him the truth.

'Because as yet she doesn't love you,' I replied.

'That's untrue,' Tom said, his voice shaking. 'You only say that because you've been jealous of her ever since she came out here.'

I forced myself to remain calm. 'Perhaps,' I answered. 'But that doesn't alter the truth.'

Tom took a long gulp of his drink. 'How can you possibly tell?' he asked.

I hesitated. I had reached dangerous ground, but I could not turn back. 'From the way she looks at you,' I replied.

Tom gave a snort of disgust. 'What a typically female remark!' he exclaimed. He began to pace up and down the room. 'You'd like to believe all you say is true, wouldn't you?' he suggested.

'No,' I answered. 'I want you to be happy.'

Suddenly I felt anger against Tom because of his apparent ingratitude. 'I want you to be happy,' I repeated, and I could not prevent the bitterness in my tone of voice. 'That seems to have been my whole purpose in life ever since you were born,' I added.

Tom swung round on his heels and looked at me. Then, slowly, he lowered his head and stared down at the carpet, as he used to do when I became cross with him when he was a child.

'I'm sorry,' Tom said. 'I've been unfair. But I won't have you saying things—or even thinking things—about Anne that aren't true.'

I realised now that he had not lowered his head because he thought he was wrong, but only because he was sorry that he had hurt my feelings. I could feel the rage burning in me once again. 'I don't *think* things,' I heard myself saying. ' I *know*. And it's best you should know too.'

'Know what?' Tom demanded.

I had now advanced far further in my attack than I had intended, but I had reached a stage from which there could be no turning back. I rose from my chair and moved towards the door and opened it.

'Just follow me,' I said.

I walked along the corridor to Anne's sitting-room. The lamp on the desk had already been lit, but the room was empty. Tom followed me and stood with his back to the grate in which logs were burning. I pointed to the bronze jar.

'*Now* what are you trying to do?' Tom asked.

'Warn you,' I answered. 'Before it's too late.'

'You always loved a mystery,' Tom said.

'There's no mystery,' I replied. 'You'll find a key in that jar. Take it out.'

Tom hesitated. Then he uptilted the jar and took the key.

'Unlock the drawer of the desk,' I told him.

Tom put in the key, turned it, and slid open the drawer.

'Take out the sheet of paper with writing on it,' I said.

'What's this nonsense about?' Tom asked.

'A poem, just a poem,' I answered. 'You can recognise Anne's writing?'

Tom took out the sheet of paper.

'Of course I can,' he replied.

'Then read the poem,' I said. 'Read it.'

Tom began to read the poem in silence. Presently, he looked up at me.

'Do you begin to understand?' I asked softly.

Tom turned away from me. I took the poem from his hand, replaced it in the drawer, locked the desk, and put back the key in the jar. Then I turned to Tom. He was glowering at me.

'Does Anne know you've read that poem?' he asked.

'Certainly not,' I answered.

'How did you know that the poem was locked in that desk?' he demanded.

'I had a strong intuition,' I replied.

'So strong that you led me straight to that drawer?' Tom enquired.

'No,' I answered. 'My intuition brought me to the drawer, and I opened it while you were out.'

'So you're prepared to spy on Anne and read her poems and letters behind her back?' Tom asked. He was shaking with anger.

'I've read none of her letters,' I replied.

'Then why did you unlock the drawer?'

'Because I wanted to find out what she was writing,' I explained. 'I thought it would help me discover what had gone wrong between the two of you.'

'You spied on her,' Tom said. 'You spied on my wife. And what have you found out? Nothing. You read poetry. Surely you don't imagine that *every* poem reflects the personal sentiments of its author?'

'Whom are you trying to persuade?' I asked.

Suddenly Tom looked bewildered and pathetic. His expression reminded me of an occasion when I had found him lost in a little wood at the end of our garden. In those days I had only to take him in my arms to comfort him, but now, because of his pride and resolution to keep a barricade firmly in position between us, it was more difficult.

'Supposing,' Tom began hesitantly, 'supposing that in some way Anne's poem explains how she feels, what am I expected to do?'

'I know you, Tom,' I replied. 'You're a strong person. But there's a part of you that's weak. There have been times when you have almost been in love, and each time your weakness has shown. But this is different.'

'You're right,' Tom said. 'I'm very much in love. There's nothing I can do about it.'

'She's wilful,' I told him. 'Anne's wilful, and I've seen it. You're her husband. You must be stronger in dealing with her. Far stronger. And *then* she may come to respect you and love you.'

7

I sit listlessly at my desk, staring out at the stableyard. On the roof, Indian house-sparrows are chirping as the afternoon sun beats down. Large, shiny black crows waddle across the yard, cawing incessantly. I gaze down at the page in front of me; then I look up again as a parakeet flies past and presently a hoopoe follows. I will not be able to go for my afternoon ride because there is a tennis-party at the Resident's house. Both Olivia Maxwell and Tom would be vexed if I did not attend. This morning it rained heavily, and the roads are muddy, so there is a chance that tennis will be cancelled. I can only hope so. A black-headed oriole has just alighted on the weather-cock on the roof of the stables. I try to make myself concentrate on its brilliant yellow plumage, but my mind keeps returning to my home in England. Two ayahs in drab-coloured saris move across the yard chattering. They carry bundles of twigs fastened together which they use as brooms. I watch them, but homesickness drives my mind away from the yard. Presently, I begin to work once again on a poem which has been in my mind for some time.

It must be breakfast time at home to-day,
    Mamma will give her orders to the cook,
    Papa is in his study with his book,
And in the stableyard my dapple grey
Leans over from her box as if to say
    'Where is my mistress?' That farewell I took
    Kissing your muzzle was our last long look.
Old friend, your mistress now is far away.

I married him as if by Royal decree,
Good regiment, a baronet-to-be,
    Rich and a gentleman, they asked no more.
They did not say his liquor-scented breath
And night embraces would be worse than death,
    Nor when he slept, how loudly he would snore.

--------◆◆◆◆--------

Three days later, as I rode along the track that led down to the
lake I saw Rodney Meadows standing by the gate of his compound.

'I was wondering when I'd see you again,' he called out. 'I
hope you'll stop for a drink?'

'I'd be delighted to,' I replied.

Rodney Meadows summoned a bearer who took Sunil and
the two horses to the back of the house. Once again I sat down
on the verandah and was given a glass of wine.

'Tell me, Mrs Carey,' Rodney Meadows said. 'Did you enjoy
the garden-party?'

'It was fun,' I replied. 'And please don't call me Mrs Carey
because it makes me feel so old.'

'Fine,' he said smiling. 'My name's Rodney. Incidentally, I
have a question to ask you. Do your husband and his sister
know that you're meeting me?'

'No,' I replied. 'I don't think they do.'

'And did you decide not to tell them because you thought
they might disapprove?' Rodney asked.

I laughed. 'I was probably quite wrong,' I said. 'But I had a
feeling they might have objected for some reason or another—
perhaps because young Sunil can hardly be called a chaperon.'

Rodney leaned forward. 'I must confess to you that your
guess was correct,' he said. 'They would object. They would
object most strongly.'

'Why should they?' I asked.

'You'll hear soon enough,' Rodney replied. 'So you might as
well be told the truth here and now.'

Rodney rose from his chair and began to walk up and down

65

the verandah. I could see that he was embarrassed. Perhaps he now regretted his decision to confide in me.

'The fact is that I don't live here all alone,' he said. 'I'm not married. I've never been able to feel the slightest passion towards any of the English ladies I've met, enchanting though many of them were. Thank heavens the feeling has been mutual. But one day by the lake I saw a young Indian girl. We became friends. Suddenly I discovered that I was in love with her. What's more, she had shown that she was fond of me. So that was how it started. She now lives here in this bungalow with me.'

Rodney paused. He stared down at his glass.

'The only reason we're not married is that *she* doesn't want to marry *me*,' Rodney continued. 'But if I married her, that would be considered a far worse crime by the English community.'

I was silent, for I could not think of anything to say without sounding stupid or patronising.

'So now you know why I'm not asked to official garden-parties,' Rodney concluded.

'I thought that one of the aims of the Empire was to abolish race prejudice,' I said.

'It may have been once,' Rodney replied. 'When the first merchant adventurers landed in India it was considered perfectly natural for a man to live with an Indian girl or even to marry her. English soldiers were encouraged to have Indian mistresses from the local town. But now all that has changed. With the advent of steamships and better transport facilities, English wives began coming out here. And from that moment any thought of racial equality vanished. Today in India you will find that the English have only two sources of contact with Indians—officers or officials who are only too prepared to sit down at the same table as an Indian if he is a Rajah, and soldiers who can pay a brief visit to Indian prostitutes in the brothels of the bazaar.'

The bearer came in with a plate of biscuits. Rodney was silent until he had left.

'But they're learning,' Rodney said. 'Little by little and every

56

day, the Indians are acquiring some form of education. And one day—it may not be for over a century—they'll throw us out. All over the world the races we've subjugated will throw us out. And on the tombstone of the British Empire may be written the words, "Lost by Snobbery".'

Rodney refilled our glasses.

'Meanwhile you may be wondering what I personally am doing to improve matters in this poor, almost hopeless country,' he said. 'I'm afraid the answer is practically nothing. The whole business is too complicated, and alas I'm far too lazy.'

'I thought a tea-planter's life was arduous.'

Rodney laughed. 'Don't you believe it!' he said. 'Not if he employs as good a *Kangany* for overseer as I have done. I'm obliged to get up at dawn, I confess. But that doesn't worry me much. I go and see my *Kangany* to make sure that everything is under control and that the coolies—male and female—have got nothing to complain about. Then I ride down to the little factory which is situated just below the stream that feeds the lake. And the rest of the day is more or less my own. It's a deliciously leisurely existence.'

Suddenly Rodney sprang to his feet.

'Would you mind meeting my Indian girl?' he asked. 'Her name's Theivaney, and she's really very sweet. She doesn't speak a word of English, but that won't matter. She'll be delighted to sit down with an English woman for once in her life.'

'I'd love to meet her,' I replied.

Rodney parted the bead curtains of the clapboard bungalow and disappeared inside. As I sipped my wine I hoped that Tom would never find out about my visits to Rodney. His disapproval would be violent. Presently Rodney came back. Following him was a young girl. Then, as I looked closer, I almost gasped. For the girl was no more than a child—certainly less than fourteen. She was very slim, and her waist was so small that one wondered it could support the rest of her fragile body. On her forehead was a red caste mark. In her small nose glittered two little gold nose-studs. The lobes of her delicate ears had been pierced, and she wore two gold earrings. Her mouth was wide; her smooth dark-brown face was dominated by her large eyes which were now peeping up at me nervously.

'This is Theivaney,' Rodney announced, and gestured to the child to sit down.

'Don't be worried because she looks so young,' Rodney said to me. 'Out here, the girls get married at the age of ten, and their husbands aren't as gentle with them as I am.'

'Are her parents alive?' I asked.

Rodney glanced towards Theivaney who was now sitting demurely in a wicker chair, her little hands clasped together, gazing at me steadily.

'I can guess what you are thinking,' Rodney said. 'You wonder why they let the girl live here. The answer is that it's all perfectly above-board. I first met Theivaney about a year ago when she was bathing in the lake. She looked so enchanting with her supple body and her huge eyes that I couldn't move. I just stood there, staring at her. And as I gazed down at her exquisite loveliness she smiled, and it was a smile of such utter complicity that I was not surprised when a second later she gave me a broad wink. The rest was comparatively simple. I found out who she was. I then sent my *Kangany* to contact her father who worked in the shop of a silver-smith in the bazaar. A few days later her father and mother came to see me. We had a long discussion together, during which it was agreed that I should give them money to buy themselves a little shop of their own. The next day I handed over the money. Theivaney appeared here in my bungalow that very night. The girl has been here ever since, and I can assure you that she is perfectly happy. Matters are arranged in this kind of way out in the East.'

'But you said the Indians were gradually learning,' I pointed out.

'Yes,' Rodney replied. 'But I don't think that any amount of learning will ever change the roots of human nature.'

'Then what is the point of them learning?' I asked.

'So that they can be free to govern themselves,' he answered. 'I don't want them to be filled with what we would call the precepts of morality. I want them to acquire knowledge so they can manage their own affairs.'

As Rodney talked, Theivaney sat perfectly still, but her eyes moved from one of us to the other, and I wondered what she was thinking. Presently she rose from her chair and crossed over to Rodney and put her arm round his neck. The gesture was both affectionate and possessive, and at that moment I realised she was genuinely devoted to him. I could now try to forget the thought of this little child lying in bed and being forced to make love to the tall middle-aged man, with his sprawling limbs and long sallow face, who sat beside me. If there had been any brutality it was now only a vague memory in her mind. What mattered to her was the present. A woman who might prove to be a rival had suddenly appeared in her home. She was instinctively jealous of her. So, in order to show her position as mistress in the household, the child began to stroke Rodney's cheek. As I watched her I began to feel a fierce envy that Theivaney had found love while I had managed to find nothing.

Rodney appeared to be rather embarrassed by the girl's overt display of affection, so I finished my glass of wine, got up to leave and said good-bye to them.

As I rode home with Sunil, still teaching him new sentences of English as I did each day, it occurred to me that Rodney, in his opinions and morals, wavered between rectitude and error like a clockwork doll.

That evening I was reading in bed when Tom came back from dining in the Mess. He kissed my forehead. I could smell the whisky on his breath. He crossed over to his dressing-room and began to take off his mess-kit.

'Are you looking forward to tomorrow?' he called out.

'Tomorrow?'

'Have you forgotten?' Tom asked, coming back into the room. 'Tomorrow you're paying a little visit to the Rajah's palace.'

'Of course,' I said. 'I'd almost forgotten.'

'Don't tell me it had slipped your memory?' Tom enquired sarcastically. 'The most handsome man in the district—even though he is coloured? What's more, Margaret can't accompany you because she's got a committee meeting.'

'He's an interesting character,' I explained. 'But I don't find him at all attractive.'

'Don't you find him romantic?' Tom asked.

'No,' I replied.

'One or two women I've known were keen on black men,' Tom said. 'But I don't advise you to try it. There wouldn't be a person in this station who would talk to you again.'

I could not prevent a gesture of disgust.

'Have I shocked you?' Tom asked.

'Perhaps not in the way you think,' I answered.

'And what does that remark mean?' he enquired.

'Let's leave it,' I replied.

Tom strode across to the bed. A towel was wound around his waist, otherwise he was naked.

'*What* did you mean?' he asked.

'Leave it,' I repeated.

'Do you think you can give orders to me?' he demanded.

'I'm sorry,' I replied. 'I should have said "Please let us leave it".'

'That's better,' Tom muttered. Then he blew out the lamp by the bed. The only light in the room now came from the fire. Tom dropped the towel and got into bed beside me. His arms grasped me. His voice was muffled as he spoke.

'I'm the Master in this house. I don't take orders. I'm the Master,' he repeated. Then he began to press against me.

'And you're going to be made to understand,' he said. 'You're going to be made to.'

❖

As I got out of the carriage beneath the portico of the palace the following afternoon I was greeted by Ashur, the Rajah's secretary. With his thin face and black suit he reminded me of a vulture. He led me into a large gilt-and-white room. As I entered, the Rajah moved forward to welcome me, and Ashur sidled out.

'I was afraid you wouldn't come,' the Rajah said.

'Why?' I asked.

The Rajah smiled at me slyly. 'I thought you might have heard that my wife is still indisposed,' he murmured.

'I'm sorry,' I told him.

'Perhaps she will be better tomorrow,' the Rajah said in a mocking whisper.

For a moment we gazed at each other in silence. I realised that as usual with women he was trying to exert his charm. But I was in no way attracted to him.

'Before we have tea, would you like to see a little of the palace?' the Rajah asked.

'I'd love to,' I replied.

The Rajah moved towards the door at the far end of the room. He gave me a little bow and held out his hand which as usual glittered with jewels.

'Please,' he said. His voice was quiet; yet, without meaning to, he made the word sound almost like a command.

We walked along a wide corridor and entered an ornate blue-and-green room. Above us was a dome overlaid with gold leaf. On a raised platform covered by a crimson carpet stood the gilt throne, encrusted with jewels. Around it the light from the muslin-curtained windows shimmered and glowed. I thought that some remark, however banal, was expected of me.

'It's all very impressive,' I said.

The Rajah smiled. 'And it's a long way from Oxford,' he added.

He moved towards another door and opened it. 'Now the way is complicated,' he explained with a gesture of apology. 'Perhaps you will excuse me if I lead?'

He walked through the door, and I followed him. We moved across a large billiards-room and entered a maze of corridors, walking along parquet floors strewn with leopard-skin rugs and flanked by a fantastic assortment of furniture. I passed beside brass-topped tables with spindly wooden legs, two upright pianos and a harmonium, damask-covered sofas, empty bird-cages, shelves of ivory carvings, and large highly coloured Indian vases. On the damp-stained walls hung full-length portraits of Indian dignitaries—some of them perhaps Rajahs, resplendent in their regalia.

'I'm afraid my forbears had little taste,' the Rajah said to me.

'The artists they employed had little talent. But I have a surprise for you.'

He moved down a narrow passage, then took the first corridor to the left. He turned to me. 'I doubt if you'd find your way back now if I left you,' he said.

'But you won't leave me,' I replied.

'No,' he answered. 'No, that's very true.'

He stopped in front of a mahogany door. 'We have arrived,' he announced.

He turned the handle and went into a room. I followed him and I gasped. For the whole apartment was furnished in eighteenth-century English style. The walls were painted an Adam green. The furniture looked as if it had been made by Chippendale and Sheraton. The pictures were also eighteenth century. One of the landscapes was by Gainsborough and the head of a young girl was by Reynolds. The mantelpiece was in the fashion of Adam. Bowls of white roses stood on the sideboards. The room was elegant and comfortable. A tea-table was laid in an alcove in the far corner. Three bearers in crimson and gold palace uniforms stood waiting beside it.

'Will you take tea?' the Rajah asked. 'Or a glass of champagne?'

'Tea, please,' I replied.

'Shall a bearer pour out?'

'No,' I said. 'I can.'

The Rajah spoke to the bearers in Tamil. They salaamed to him and then to me and left us. At that moment I gazed out of the window in astonishment. For through the lace curtains I could see an English park stretching away into the distance. Grass-land rolled smoothly past vast oaks until it reached a long lake fringed with willows. The Rajah saw my look of amazement and laughed.

'Go to the window and look closer,' he told me.

I walked across and looked out. Some ten feet from the window was the park—painted as a fresco on a wall.

'It's a trick of the light from the ceiling,' the Rajah explained. 'I designed it entirely myself.'

I wondered why the Rajah who had obviously been unhappy

in England should take such pains to re-create the facsimile of a room in an English country house. Perhaps it was some special form of envy. I sat down and began to pour out the tea.

'For me—without milk or sugar,' the Rajah said. Suddenly he clapped his hands together and laughed. 'What a domestic scene!' he exclaimed. 'Quite perfect. I must try to make it last.'

I smiled. 'How could you do that?'

'For instance, by arranging for you to be in this room at this time every day of the week,' he answered.

For a moment his wolfish look had returned.

Then it was gone, and the lines of his face were set pleasantly once again.

'I'm afraid that arrangement wouldn't be possible,' I said.

'Why not?'

'I have a husband.'

'And I have a wife,' the Rajah said. 'But that problem could, I daresay, be settled in time. And then, if such an odd idea should ever cross your mind, you could join me.'

I laughed. I did not believe that he was being serious. Not for an instant. 'Why should you ever imagine that I would dream of leaving my husband?' I asked.

'Rumours,' he answered.

'Then your rumours have misled you,' I told him.

For a moment he was silent. He had joined the tips of his fingers together and was staring down at them. Then he looked up at me. 'Anne,' he said, 'do you understand?'

'No,' I replied. 'No, I'm sure I don't.'

He began playing with a sapphire ring on his left hand, sliding it up and down his finger.

'I think you do understand,' he said, smiling. 'Or perhaps you are afraid to understand. So I will put it a little more clearly.' He paused. Once again he looked down at his hands, then let them fall on to his lap.

'For all you know, I might conceivably be interested,' he said slowly. 'I might be making a devious attempt to intimate that I might want you as my wife. Who knows? People can be attracted to each other at first sight—or so the poets tell us. And I'm informed that you write poetry. So let us suppose

63

that I have fallen in love with you. Do you object to the supposition? Suppose I loved you from the moment I first saw you on the lawn of this palace. What could I do about it?'

He paused and took a sip from his cup. He was smiling, and I still believed he was—in his rather awkward way—trying to tease me.

'What could I do?' he repeated. 'Very little at first. I am an Indian with a black skin, so I must be careful—even though I am a Rajah. I have had successes in my time, but now I must move cautiously. For you are unlike the wives of the other officers in Telacamund. So I am obliged to move *very* carefully. Accordingly, I ask you to tea. And even then I am afraid to tell you the truth.'

I glanced at his face. To my astonishment I saw that he was being serious. I was dismayed. Then I remembered his reputation of having charmed several English ladies in his time. I tried to smile. 'Do you often propose to girls who are married?' I asked.

'Once,' he answered. 'Once at Oxford. The girl worked in a bar.'

'What did she say?'

'Nothing. She just threw my beer at my face.'

'The tea's too good,' I told him. 'Besides, I don't like to spoil your Aubusson carpet.'

He spoke very quietly. 'I give you the carpet,' he said. 'I give it to you as my first present.'

'Thank you,' I replied. 'But you know that I can't accept it.'

He got up and walked to the window and gazed at the landscape painted on the wall. 'Your husband sleeps with you every night,' he said. 'Yet you are still unawakened.'

I had been mildly amused when I had thought that in his gauche way he was making fun of me. But now that I knew he was no longer bothering to pretend that he was speaking in jest, I was angry.

'More servants' gossip?' I asked.

The Rajah turned away from the window. 'I can see with my own eyes,' he replied.

He moved across to me. 'You must understand,' he said. 'You must.'

'Why must I?' I asked him.

'Because I love you.'

'When you've only met me once?' I asked.

'I love you,' he replied. 'I loved you from the first instant I saw you.'

As he now stared at me, I felt he was exerting all the will-power he could summon to attract me to him. But I was only aware of his lean, rather arrogant face pointed towards me. I could feel not a trace of desire for him. In fact there was now something about his extreme intensity which produced in me a feeling of disgust. And when he stretched out his arm to take my hand I could not help moving away from him.

'You're kind,' he said. 'You would hurt no one willingly. But if it were possible—if it were possible without hurting anyone—then perhaps, one day, would you, Anne? Would you one day think of me?'

Slowly I shook my head.

'You don't want me?' he asked.

'I know I should be honoured,' I answered. 'I suppose I am. But I'm afraid I could never accept.'

I could hear my voice speaking. I could watch his eager face as he listened to me. Yet somehow I did not feel that it was I who was speaking, for the whole scene in this imitation drawing-room with the imitation park, which I could glimpse through the lace-covered windows, had taken on a dream-like quality. I suppose it was for this reason that I was not afraid of him in any way, though I knew that I was alone with him and trapped. His forehead was glistening as he stared at me. His hands were now quivering. The words came jerking awkwardly from his mouth.

'You wouldn't,' he said. 'You wouldn't perhaps consider it?'

'No,' I heard myself saying. 'Neither as a husband nor a lover.'

For a moment he gazed at me as if he had not heard what I had said. Then his shoulders twitched, and his features became distorted. Quickly he covered his face with his hands. He got up and moved away from me. His voice when he spoke was almost inaudible.

'You say that because my skin is coloured,' he muttered.

'For no such stupid reason, I promise you,' I replied.

But he was not listening to me. His hands when he let them fall from his face were still quivering, and his eyes were red.

'Now let me tell you the truth,' he cried out. 'Let me tell you that English women—despite the colour of my skin—not only common women, but ladies of rank and title—have offered themselves to me like cheap prostitutes. They have begged me. They have entreated me. They have cajoled me with every device of charm that they could muster. They have gone down on their knees to me. They have wanted to perform the acts of whores from the bazaar.'

As he screeched out the obscene words, his face had grown a strange livid colour, and his mouth was wet with froth. I got up from my chair. The scene in which I was taking part had ceased to be a dream. A gob of spittle had fallen from his mouth on to his silk tunic, and this yellow gob, for some reason, had become in my eyes more real than anything else in the contrived room. I forced my voice to sound firm. I controlled the fear which I could now feel invading me.

'I would like to leave now,' I told him.

He hesitated. Then he crossed the room and pulled the bell-rope. When he turned round to me, he was still trembling, but his mouth was no longer grimacing and I could see that he was growing calmer. My nightmarish fear that he would break down into some terrible fit of madness was now receding.

'May I put to you one question?' he asked.

'Certainly,' I answered.

I was now making a strong effort to control myself.

'Is there no one else?' he asked me.

'I'm married,' I said.

His red-flecked eyes were glaring at my face. 'I meant,' he began slowly, 'is there another man?'

'No,' I replied.

He was still breathing heavily. 'I tell you this,' he muttered, with a slight catch in his throat. 'If ever I found there was another man, he would be sorry for it.'

I was now only conscious of my anger. 'And as you once reminded me,' I said, 'we're far away from Oxford.'

Suddenly his head twisted away from me as if he were a puppet whose strings had been abruptly wrenched. His fingers began to squirm and writhe together.

'Thank you for reminding me,' he hissed out at me.

As he spoke, the door opened and a bearer came in and salaamed to us. For a second, the Rajah seemed unaware of the man's presence. Then, with an effort, he clasped his hands together to control their twitching. Slowly he raised his head. As he looked towards the bearer, he assumed his attitude of a Rajah once again. He spoke briefly to the bearer in Tamil. Then he turned back to me.

'I have told the man to escort you to your carriage,' he said.

The bearer opened the door, and I moved towards it. For some reason that I could not explain to myself I had an idiotic desire to make some remark to break the nightmare which seemed to have enveloped us. Perhaps we might yet find a manner of regaining a normal atmosphere.

'Thank you for showing me the palace,' I blurted out stupidly.

The Rajah acknowledged my remark with a slight inclination of his head.

'Thank you for reminding me that I'm still a mere nigger,' he replied.

He swung away from me and walked across to the window. He was still gazing at the painted landscape as I left the room.

8

My committee meeting finished early and I hurried back home. Obviously, Anne had locked the drawer of her desk because she was determined that we should not read any of her poems. I would like to have been able to respect her desire for this personal secret. But I thought that for Tom's sake I must force myself to keep an eye on the poems the girl wrote in order to help him in his relationship with her. So as soon as I returned to the house I went into Anne's little sitting-room and unlocked the drawer. I knew I was safe, for I had discovered that Anne had left a few minutes ago to have tea with the Rajah and his wife at the palace.

The beginning of the poem was innocent enough but the last six lines amounted to a direct attack on Tom. I was revolted by her crudity in mentioning the snoring and the smell of liquor on his breath. Since Anne would not be returning from the palace for at least an hour I took the poem with me into the drawing-room because I intended to show it to Tom at the first opportunity. I realised, of course, that from every point of view I would be making a terrible mistake if I tried to break up the marriage. But I was determined that Tom must somehow be awakened from the idyllic dream in which he now appeared to spend his days in love for his young wife. I was equally determined that Anne must be taught her proper place. There is no vice about Anne—I am perfectly sure of that. She has charm. More important still, she has an essentially sweet nature. But her high faluting notions need curbing, and her obstinacy needs to be controlled.

While I was working out the household accounts Tom came back from the barracks. When the bearer had given him his chotapeg I showed him the sonnet. Tom read it in silence. Then he finished his drink.

'When Anne wrote that poem she was home-sick,' he said. 'And she was annoyed with me. That's all there is to it.'

Poor dear Tom! I knew what an intense effort he was making to convince himself that all was well with his marriage. I felt so sorry for him that for a moment I considered whether I should now leave him to the peace of his delusions. But then I reminded myself that if he persisted in his wilfully blind ignorance, his final awakening to the truth would be all the more bitter.

' "Liquor-scented breath and night embraces worse then death," ' I quoted. 'Is that the poem of a contented wife?' I asked him.

'Anne was annoyed with me when she wrote those lines,' Tom replied.

'She's disloyal to you,' I told him. 'And in your heart you know the reason why. She doesn't as yet love you.'

'Give her time,' Tom answered.

'And let her have an affair with the Rajah in the meanwhile?' I asked.

Tom managed to smile. 'My dear Margaret,' he exclaimed, 'what nonsense you do talk! That pompous little coolie! Anne wouldn't dream of it. Besides, she'd never be unfaithful to me.'

I looked at the clock on the mantelpiece. 'She's been gone for quite a while,' I said.

'She has indeed,' Tom answered. 'I expect she's called on Marjorie Russell on her way home.'

'Why?'

'Because I asked her to,' Tom replied. 'The regimental wives of this station think that Anne is conceited because she has little or nothing to do with them. That must stop.'

An outsider listening to this vigorously delivered speech might have supposed that Tom was a strong-willed and firm—almost brutally firm—character, and his soldierly figure and the sternness of his handsome face would have borne out this opinion. Perhaps I was the only person in the world who knew that his bluff manners and severe expression concealed an inward shyness and an unusual sensitivity.

'You're besotted with her, aren't you?' I said quietly.

Tom glared at me. 'I'm very much in love,' he replied. Then he gave a little sigh.

'Anne knows that,' I told him. 'And she takes advantage accordingly.'

Tom checked an impatient gesture of his hand. 'How?' he enquired.

'Why did you give her the mare?' I asked him.

'Because it made her happy,' Tom answered. 'Besides, I'd always intended to give her a horse as a present.'

'What if she uses the mare to ride over to the palace?' I asked.

'Your whole idea's disgusting and ridiculous,' Tom told me. 'It's completely unthinkable.'

'Is it?' I replied. 'Both of us know of at least two women on this station who have nearly fallen to his allures, however flashy they may be.'

'And another thing,' Tom added. 'Anne never goes out without a syce, does she?'

'Young Sunil!' I exclaimed. 'Anne could bribe him without the slightest difficulty. I know these ex-mission-school boys. I know it's most unlikely. But, alas, it's not wholly impossible.'

'I think it is *utterly* impossible,' Tom answered. 'But we can find out if anything is going on easily enough. I can put a man to watch that gaudy gin-palace.'

'Perhaps,' I replied. 'Perhaps you should.'

I took the sonnet and went to Anne's sitting-room and locked it in her desk. A few moments later, when Tom and I were reading the newspapers from Madras, Anne returned to the house. I thought she looked tired and pale. Tom and I had agreed that it was essential I should disguise any uneasy suspicion I might entertain.

'Did you call on Marjorie?' Tom asked her.

'Yes,' Anne replied. 'I played the part of a dutiful regimental wife for almost an hour, so that now I feel quite exhausted.'

'How was the Rajah?' Tom asked.

'He showed me around the palace,' Anne replied, 'and he gave me tea. But it seems that his wife is still ill, so I left as soon as I decently could.'

'I shan't let you visit the palace again,' Tom told her.

For an instant Anne hesitated. 'I was disappointed not to meet the Ranee,' she said. 'I'd looked forward to talking to her. She would have been the first Indian lady I'd have met.'

I was watching Anne closely. She seemed perfectly composed. She picked up a paper and began to read it. For a while there was silence. The room was growing cold. I was glad when Belur came in and lit the fire. I took up my paper once again. As usual it contained reports of disaster. 'Three soldiers from the Fourteenth Hussars have been drowned in the monsoon floods up north,' I read out to them.

'This paper says that over one hundred Indians were swept away by the floods, and over a thousand are now homeless,' Anne announced.

'Yes,' I said. 'But Indians get used to the strange ways of Providence.'

'I wonder,' Anne murmured.

'You mustn't suppose that the masses in this country are anything like the Rajah,' Tom said gently. 'After all, at least he has a veneer of English education.'

'Yet he still feels an outcast when he's with us,' Anne answered.

'Because he's an Indian,' Tom told her. 'He's aware of the barrier between us. He knows that all the wealth in the world won't bridge that great divide.'

'But surely one day . . .' Anne began.

'Don't get any romantic notions about the Indians,' Tom said. 'If your life were spent helping natives, the enthusiasm and novelty would soon wear off. You'd find there was a vast gulf fixed between yourself and men who would never admit you to their home-life, men who would consider themselves and their wives and daughters insulted if you even sat down at their own table, men who in their innermost heart wouldn't be sad if every Christian in this country were driven into the sea.'

'In time it must change,' Anne stated.

'In time what must change?' Tom asked. 'With our relief organisations and our charities and hospitals, aren't we doing enough already?'

'Surely there must be something more we can do to relieve the ghastly poverty of this place,' Anne answered.

Tom tapped the side of the table in a movement of impatience. 'Your ideas are completely wrong,' he told Anne. 'You have no idea of reality. Certainly it's the duty of the Government to save life, but it's not bound to maintain the labour population at their normal level of subsistence.'

'Anne's not only worried about the economic situation,' I explained to Tom. 'She wants us to mix with the natives.'

'What rot!' Tom cried, turning to Anne. 'Is this the result of your tea-party with the Rajah?'

'I don't know,' Anne replied.

'As I told you, I'm not going to let you visit him alone again,' Tom said. 'Did he show you his "English room"?'

Once again Anne hesitated. I found these hesitations of Anne's that evening very odd. I couldn't understand the reason for them.

'Yes,' Anne answered. 'I found it entrancing.'

Tom scowled. I could see that he was growing angry.

'I daresay,' he answered. 'But did you know there was a hidden door which leads to a room—not quite so English?'

'No,' Anne replied.

'I've heard rumours that what goes on in that little room isn't very pleasant,' Tom said. 'The Rajah's civilised manners don't extend to his secret room, I can assure you.'

Tom turned away from Anne and stared at me grimly.

'And now,' he said, 'I think it's time for us to go and dress for dinner.'

He crossed the room, opened the door, and held it open for Anne and myself.

9

Yesterday evening I completely lost my temper with Tom for the first time.

'Everything I now do,' I cried out to him, 'everything I now say seems to displease you. But what have I done wrong? Nothing.'

Tom came over to me in our bedroom and took my face between his hands and stared into my eyes in silence.

'Nothing,' he said, speaking so softly that it was as if he were talking to himself. 'Nothing. You've done nothing wrong, and I love you very much.'

———◆———

I now seem to live in a strange kind of limbo. One day slides by after another. Twice a week I am driven to the beautiful old library to change my books. Often I accompany Margaret on her shopping expeditions. When we are in the market and I see the radishes and cabbages, the apples and pears and raspberries, I feel that I am at home in England once again. Blackcurrants, peaches and strawberries on the table; the rain streaking the window-panes; hollyhocks and damask roses in the garden; English fir-trees and oaks in the country beyond the compound—all of them conspire to give me the illusion of home. And yet I know that in the narrow streets of the bazaar, Indian men and women and children, clustered together like a swarm of bees, are living in poverty and squalor. Jackals, panthers, and leopards lurk in the fir-topped hills.

The happiest moment of my day is when I go out riding in the late afternoon. The brief showers of rain have almost stopped, and I can give Sunil the English lessons I promised him. I have not called on Rodney Meadows again, because I am afraid that Tom may somehow get to hear of my visits to him, and I do not want to give Tom an excuse to make a jealous scene. I want the days to glide by smoothly and effortlessly.

I was riding along a track through the wood, and Sunil was following me in silence. I had discussed with him some of the books I had secretly lent him from the library—books of short stories which he liked, and an English phrase-book—but our conversation had come to an end. The air was close; the horses were walking slowly. High up in the trees marvellously coloured parrots were screeching and grey monkeys chattering. Suddenly my mind switched back to my former home, and I saw myself wandering across the lawn to the lavender beds, while my spaniel, Carrie, frisked around beside me. At the end of the garden I saw my mother, leaning on my father's arm, and they called out to me in greeting. With them was my cousin Luke who had come to stay for the summer vacation from Cambridge.

I must have been sixteen at the time, and Luke was nineteen. He was tall and slim, with long russet hair and large green eyes which gave him a romantic look. Even as a child I had found him insipid and remote, and I'd been dismayed when my parents had told me that he was coming to stay with us for a few weeks. He had a weak chest and his father, who was a clergyman in Birmingham, had thought that the air of our farm in Berkshire would improve his condition. I found him shy and awkward. But gradually, as the days passed, he became less tongue-tied, and soon, when we went out together for walks across the Downs, his last traces of shyness seemed to vanish. He began to speak to me freely about the matters closest to his heart. There were two passions in his life— Socialism and poetry.

74

At Cambridge he had made friends with a Don who was a founder member of the newly formed Fabian Society, a small group of Socialists who rejected the concept of class struggle and violent revolution and believed in the gradual, but inevitable, spread of collectivist ideas throughout the country. Luke was appalled by the inequality which existed, and still exists, in England. He was disgusted by the poverty he had seen in his father's parish in Birmingham. He had joined a local organisation which tried to alleviate the suffering of the poor. Presently, I realised that one of the reasons his father had sent him to our farm in Berkshire was because Luke had been working overhard and his health was growing worse.

Luke was particularly revolted by the evils of child labour. He gave me terrible descriptions of the ill-treatment of children and of the exploitation of them. I sensed that there were examples of cruelty yet more horrible which he could have told me about, but which he refrained from doing so for fear of shocking me.

As he talked, I would sometimes glance up at him. He strode beside me, walking so fast that I could scarcely keep up with him, his russet hair flowing in the breeze, his face alight with indignation. Gradually his eagerness and sincerity made me grow fond of him. When he spoke of the day which he was convinced would surely come, when all the iniquities would be swept away from England's pleasant land, his whole countenance became transformed by the intensity of his ideal. I realised that he was indeed a handsome young man.

It was Luke who encouraged my love of poetry. He tried to persuade me to show him some of the verses I had written, but I refused because I was afraid he would think them inept and childish. The poet whose work Luke read most frequently was William Blake. Even now, three years later, I can see Luke, in his rough tweed jacket and thick corduroy trousers, staring across the Downs—his long, soft hair moving gently in the breeze and a strange look of yearning in his green eyes. I can hear his voice as he read to me from *Songs of Innocence*.

When my mother died I was young,
And my father sold me while yet my tongue
Could scarcely cry "'weep! 'weep! 'weep! 'weep!'
So your chimneys I sweep, and in soot I sleep.

There's little Tom Dacre, who cried when his head,
That curl'd like a lamb's back, was shav'd: so I said
'Hush, Tom! never mind it, for when your head's bare
You know that the soot cannot spoil your white hair.'

———◆◆◆◆———

Sometimes Luke would wander off on his own, whilst I would
do my household chores. One afternoon, I had been helping
our cook to make strawberry jam. It was a very warm day and
when I had finished I decided to go for a walk. I entered the
wood at the end of our garden. The air was close, and the
wood was very quiet. I was trying to work out the last lines
of a sonnet, so I walked slowly. Gleaming like a mirror through
the trees ahead of me, I could see the water of our pond which,
it was rumoured, held carp. We had never, however, seen one.
I approached the pond quietly.

I heard a splash as if someone had thrown a pebble into the
pond. I walked on. Then I stopped, for I saw that someone
was swimming in the pond. As I looked at the head raised
above the muddy water I knew that it was Luke. At that
moment he swam towards the bank quite close to me and
clambered out of the water. As he stood sunning himself, my
first instinct was to turn and go. But I was afraid to move in
case some sound alerted him of my presence and he should
think that I had been watching him. I remained motionless.

I knew, of course, that it was wrong of me to stare at a
naked man. But I could not stop gazing at him because,
undressed, he seemed a different person. He always used to
wear a heavy, coarse jacket and thick cord trousers, and
because of his clothing I had stupidly imagined that the texture
of his skin would be equally coarse, but his body was smooth
and hairless. His skin was milk-white and unblemished. Naked

he was even slimmer than I had imagined him to be. As he stood there, with his arms outstretched to the sun, he reminded me more of a child than of a man. While I stood watching him he joined his hands together and dived into the pond. At that moment I moved away quickly and walked back to the house.

A few evenings later my mother was unwell and retired to bed early, so Luke and I dined alone with my father. When I think of our farmhouse I can remember most clearly the little dining-room, with its oak-panelled walls and oak refectory table on which at night stood two George II candelabra which my father had inherited. I can see my father sitting at the head of the table, the candlelight glowing on his brick-red face which contrasted pleasantly with his prematurely white hair. He was a bluff kindly man, well disposed towards everyone he met, cheerful and benign. He was conservative by nature, and I knew that some of Luke's Fabian views would probably shock him, so I had warned Luke accordingly. That particular evening, however, perhaps because he had drunk several glasses of the strong home-brewed cider which my father always served, Luke became loquacious. My father had mentioned that earlier that evening he had ridden across to the Manor House to call on Tom's father, Sir John Carey, who was his landlord.

'Doesn't it rile you to think that you don't own the land that you farm?' Luke asked him suddenly as we sat drinking coffee at the end of the meal.

'Rile me?' my father repeated gently. 'No, I wouldn't say that it riled me.'

'But you don't own a single acre of it,' Luke persisted.

'There are various forms of land tenure,' my father pointed out. 'I'm secure in my tenancy so long as I pay my rent.'

'But why should you pay Sir John Carey money when it is your labour that has made the land fruitful and profitable?' Luke demanded.

'Because Sir John owns the land,' my father replied. 'And he owns this house, and he's responsible for its upkeep. If the roof falls in he has to put on a new one. That's part of our agreement. He's my landlord. But I really don't see why that should worry me. There have been landlords since the world began—or so we're told.'

Luke threw back his head; his hair seemed golden in the candlelight.

'That's just it,' he cried. 'The whole system is antiquated and unjust. Why should Sir John live in luxury up at the Manor on the sweat of all his tenants and labourers?'

'What is the alternative?' my father asked.

'The alternative's very simple,' Luke replied. 'The alternative is that the land should be divided up so that each man who wants to be a farmer should have a parcel of land of his own to farm.'

'Would he have a plough?' my father asked. 'Would he have horses to draw the plough? Would he have cattle? Would he have granaries and stables? If not, who would give him all the equipment he would need? No country in the world could afford it. The whole idea is impractical. And how is the man going to run his farm? Is he going to have labourers? And if so, what about *their* parcel of land? The whole concept makes no sense at all. And if these are the kind of notions they teach nowadays at Cambridge, I'm afraid my poor brother is wasting his money.'

Abruptly, Luke pushed back his chair, rose from the table, and left the room. My father smiled ruefully at me.

'Evidently at Cambridge they not only teach false notions,' he said. 'They neglect to teach their pupils good manners.'

'Luke looked very tired tonight,' I replied. 'And he obviously doesn't realise how strong the cider is. I'm sure he didn't mean to be rude.'

'Perhaps you're right,' my father answered. 'All the same, I'm a little worried about that young man.'

'He seems far healthier since he came here,' I pointed out.

'It's not his health I'm worried about,' my father said. 'I'm worried because I think he's a very emotional young man full of romantic ideas.'

'Why should that worry you?' I asked.

'Because I wouldn't like him to have any romantic notions about you, my dear Anne,' my father answered.

I laughed in astonishment.

'But he doesn't,' I said. 'Far from it. He may have romantic ideas, but there's nothing romantic about his attitude towards me I can promise you.'

'Don't be too sure,' my father told me. 'I've seen the way he sometimes looks at you. And I must tell you that even if the pair of you waited until you have both attained the age of discretion I should consider that such an alliance would be extremely unsuitable.'

Once again I laughed.

'You don't need to worry,' I said. 'Really you don't. Besides, I'm certain that if Luke had any such feelings towards me I'd be aware of them by now. As it is, we're just friends and that's all there is to it.'

'I'm glad of your assurance,' my father replied. 'You're a sensible girl, my dear Anne. And I know I can trust you not to be imprudent.'

That evening, as I lay in bed, I thought over what my father had said. I now remembered that sometimes when we were walking together Luke would take my hand. I had thought that this was only a gesture of friendship, but I now began to wonder if indeed Luke did feel some romantic affection for me. Then I recalled what I had seen beside the pond. I remembered the smoothness of Luke's milk-white skin and the gracefulness of his movements. For the first time I became very much aware that Luke, with his russet hair and slender body, was lying in the room next to mine. I could picture him motionless in his bed, staring up at the ceiling as I myself was doing. Would he be thinking of me, I wondered, or would his mind still be disturbed by his argument with my father? Once more I could see the whiteness of his shoulders as he raised his arms to dive into the pond. Suddenly a terrible craving came over me and I longed to stroke Luke's skin and to hold him in my arms. But I knew that this desire must be wrong, for it was a betrayal of my love for Tom. I became ashamed of this yearning which, for an instant, had almost overwhelmed me.

In the days that followed I avoided Luke as much as I could —partly because of what my father had said and partly because

I was still ashamed of my transient moment of attraction towards him. Luke apologised to my father for his rudeness; my father told him not to be a fool and to forget all about it; and though I sometimes looked at Luke out of the corner of my eyes I could see nothing in his expression which could justify my father's suspicions. Therefore when, after lunch on a fine day a fortnight later, Luke asked me if I would go out for a walk with him I accepted without hesitation. However, as we made our way towards the Downs I soon became aware that Luke's manner was strained and restive. He was no longer at ease with me and seemed to find conversation difficult. He would start to talk about his life at Cambridge and break off in mid-sentence, then walk on again in silence. It was as if he had something on his mind that he wanted to say to me, but didn't know quite how to begin.

The afternoon was unusually hot. Presently—to my surprise —he led the way down the hillside into a deep ravine which was thickly covered by ferns.

'The heat's stifling today,' he said. 'Let's sit down.'

Obediently I sat down beside him.

'It's interesting how innocent girls of your age and class can be in this day and age,' Luke blurted out suddenly.

'You say "your class," ' I told him, 'but in fact, you and I are obviously of the same class since we're first cousins.'

'I don't *feel* we belong to the same class,' Luke replied.

'You may not feel it,' I answered, 'but the fact remains that we do. We're both middle class, and that's the plain fact of it. Besides, I wouldn't describe myself as unusually innocent.'

'You don't even know the facts of life,' Luke announced.

'If you mean what I think you do,' I said, 'then you're wrong. Quite apart from what my parents have told me, I've lived on a farm all my life. You can't live for long on a farm and *not* understand the facts of nature.'

Luke gazed at me with his large green eyes.

'So you do know,' he said. 'You do understand.'

'I expect so,' I answered.

'Do you ever think about it?' Luke asked. 'Does it ever worry you?'

'Yes,' I answered. 'I suppose it worries all young people at times.'

'But have you ever wanted to do anything about it?' Luke asked.

'Don't you think this conversation is becoming rather unseemly?' I said.

'There!' he cried out suddenly. 'There it is—the false, bogus, hypocritical puritanism inherent in almost every member of the middle class. Can't you see that you're afraid to see the truth? You're afraid to recognise even within yourself the yearnings and passions of your body. You douse your desire with a fountain of moral platitudes and religious precepts. You'll never allow all that is good and natural to spring up inside you—because you're frightened of the consequences. You're frightened you might become a human being instead of a straight-laced puppet.'

'Have you finished?' I asked.

'No,' Luke answered. 'I have not finished. Just let me tell you this. If you had been born into the working class and you went out with a young man of whom you became fond, you'd lie with him and you'd make love to him and you'd unleash your nature and know real happiness at last.'

'And then have to marry the lout because I was with a child,' I added, thinking of one of our dairy maids.

'Perhaps,' Luke replied. 'And perhaps you'd experience joy every single night that you lay with him.'

'I don't like this kind of talk,' I told Luke. 'I'm going.'

But Luke grasped my wrist.

'No,' he said. 'You'll stay and you'll listen because you've simply got to understand. Blake puts it as wonderfully as any-one I know: "Abstinence sows sand all over—The ruddy limbs and flaming hair," '—Luke paused and stared into my eyes. He was trembling with emotion—' "But Desire gratified —Plants fruits of life and beauty there." Now do you under-stand?' he concluded.

'Yes,' I answered. 'I understand. And now I think I should leave you.'

I tried to get up, but I could not move, for Luke still held me. His left arm still grasped my wrist, but his right hand had begun to stroke my throat above the opening of my dress. When he spoke, now, his voice was so soft and so gentle that it might have been another person speaking.

'Anne, please don't go,' he murmured. 'Please listen to me. Please. Anne, I love you. I'm in love with you. Very much in love. And I want to make love to you here in this little valley where no one can see us.'

'No,' I told him. 'Luke, you know that it's impossible.'

But as I spoke he had gently drawn me down to the ground and now lay holding me in his right arm. He thrust his left hand deep into the pocket of his corduroy trousers. He laid down and kissed my cheek. His lips were very soft. Then he lay beside me so that his cheek was touching mine. At last I could feel the smoothness of his skin. I knew that in lying beside him I was doing wrong, but in a curious way I still thought of him as I had seen him by the pond—looking more like a child than a man. I felt, as we lay there stretched out on the grass between the tall ferns, that we were more like two children than lovers. For a while we rested there in silence. But then I felt his right hand moving. Suddenly he touched the skin of my breast. I did not move.

Thus we remained for a few minutes. I noticed that his left hand was still deep in the pocket of his trousers and I could not understand why. Suddenly Luke gave a little sob. Violently he withdrew his right hand from my breast. Quickly he tore himself away from me and rose to his feet, only to fling himself down again a few yards away from me where he began sobbing passionately. I was so astonished that I could not move. I did not understand the reason for his tears, nor did the words that he gasped out remove my incomprehension.

'It's no good,' he sobbed. 'It's no good. I should have known.'

His hands clasped his chest and his face was drawn in anguish as if he was suffering some ghastly torture.

'Are you in pain?' I asked.

'No,' he gasped out. 'I'm not in pain. But please go. Please leave me alone. I'll find my own way back to the farm, I promise you.'

I got up and went over to him. I loosened the collar of his shirt and put my hand on his chest because I was afraid he had had a heart attack. He was sweating heavily but his heartbeats were regular. Suddenly I realised that at last I was touching the skin of his body. I withdrew my hand.

'Promise you'll come straight back to the farm,' I said to him.

'I promise,' he muttered.

I left him there, stretched out like a crumpled doll. The sun glinted on his russet hair.

Luke returned to the farm before sunset. An hour before dawn the following morning I heard him get up from his bed in the room next to mine. I heard him moving about. I realised that he was packing his bag. Later, I heard him creeping along the landing.

When my parents came down to breakfast they found a polite letter from Luke in which he thanked them for their hospitality and told them that now his health had improved he felt it was his duty to resume his social work in Birmingham.

I never heard from Luke again. But my uncle wrote to tell us that after a fortnight of work in the social settlement Luke had collapsed and had been sent to hospital. However, he recovered in time to return to Cambridge. He had graduated with Honours and was now on the staff of a small socialist magazine.

Sometimes, when Tom is unusually brutal in his lovemaking, I think about Luke and I remember him standing by the pond, and sometimes I cannot stop myself from wondering if I would not feel the joy he had promised me I would experience if I had that slim, child-like body resting in my arms instead of the man who was thrusting into me.

My mind now flicked back to the wood through which I was riding with Sunil following in silence and to the sun slanting through the trees and to the incessant cawing of the crows. A monkey scampered away, a hand held on its hip, and disappeared into the undergrowth. And as I watched the monkey vanish, what I can only describe as frenzy descended on my mind. The track through which we were riding became distorted. The trees assumed horrifying shapes and seemed to grow closer together. The air became fetid; the whole wood was now full of menace. The rays of the sun held anger. I felt a wild urge to escape from the dark foliage which appeared to be pressing in on me. And my mare, Cara, somehow became infected by my mood. Or perhaps it was I who urged her to break into a canter and then into a gallop, for I felt that the mare also wanted to escape from the threat of the oppressive wood. She began to gallop fast. Vaguely I was aware of branches slashing across my face and of Sunil galloping behind me. Perhaps for a moment he thought that my horse had bolted. Ahead of me I could see that the track was strewn with boulders, but Cara still raced forward, and I made no attempt to hold her in. I was heedless of danger; I believed that both of us were infected by the same frantic need to escape from the twisted, grotesque trees, deformed and sinuous, which menaced us with their mis-shapened branches. The ground was now uncertain and treacherous, but the mare still galloped on, and I could hear that Sunil was now far behind. Then, abruptly, ahead of us I saw a clearing, and, as I became aware of it, instantaneously the madness that had filled my mind lifted away from me. At the same moment the mare slowed down and came to a halt in this little glade in the wood.

A few seconds later Sunil caught up with us. He reined in his horse and stared at me. I was still dazed. Gradually I noticed his anxious eyes watching me. I tried to smile. Both horses had now come to a standstill. They were panting for breath and covered in a froth of sweat. Sunil dismounted. Swiftly he slid the rein over his horse's head and looped it over a tree-stump. Then he walked over to me and cupped his hands beneath my side-saddle. In silence I dismounted. Sunil led my horse to another tree and tethered her. I now felt in a kind of stupor of numbness.

'Thank you, Sunil,' I heard myself say.

As I gazed vaguely around the little clearing we had reached I saw a grass-covered bank. I slipped off my riding-jacket and sat down on the grass and leaned back in exhaustion. I watched Sunil as he removed his gloves and took off the saddles of the two horses. He spoke softly in Tamil to Cara as he began to rub her down with wisps of grass. For a moment I closed my eyes. When I opened them, Sunil was stroking his chestnut horse and crooning to it soothingly. For a while he was completely absorbed. Then, when he was satisfied that his work was done and that the horses were calm, he straightened his tunic and took up a position a few paces from the bank on which I lay and stood there alert but motionless. This was obviously what he had been taught to do. For a time I watched him, standing there rigid, with his hands behind his back and his feet parted. But presently I felt that I must break the silence.

'I don't know what happened,' I began.

'The horse run away, Memsahib,' Sunil replied.

'No,' I said. 'It was my fault. I'm sorry for it, Sunil.'

'I am your syce,' Sunil answered. 'I see that Memsahib come to no harm.'

I no longer felt dazed, but a pleasant sleepiness was covering my mind like a cloak.

'I have rubbed down the horses.' I heard Sunil's voice from what seemed a long distance away. 'In a while, when Memsahib is rested, we ride back.'

I looked up at him. He was still standing in his fixed position. His face, as often, looked a little sad. His lips were slightly parted so that I could see his teeth which seemed absurdly white against the black satin of his skin. It worried me that someone as slim and as lithe as Sunil should stand so stiffly.

'Sunil,' I said.

'Memsahib?'

'You needn't stand there,' I told him. 'Sit down and rest yourself.'

'I'm not tired,' Sunil replied in his oddly hoarse voice which sounded as if it had only recently broken.

'You can still sit down,' I said.

Sunil hesitated. Then, nervously, he sat himself down on the bank at the left of me, so that he was quite near. Neither of us spoke. But though I did not look at him I was aware that he was staring at me. From his body came a fresh rather feral smell that was pleasant and seemed somehow in conformity with the simplicity of the glade. A small monkey flitted across the clearing and sprang up into a tree. The noise of birds twittering in the leaves above our heads was loud, yet I could hear the sound of Sunil's breathing. Gradually I became very much aware of his presence. Though I did not turn to look at him, I was conscious of this supple boy with his smooth ebony-black skin sitting beside me. I now began to fancy that I could not only smell the warmth of his young body but I could even feel on the skin of my face the heat that came from him. For some reason I had never been so intensely sensitive to my surroundings before—and, more particularly, to my companion. I knew that for some reason Sunil had begun to sweat; I had also noticed the fact that he was now breathing faster and more deeply. The movement of his hand was so quiet that if I had not reached this acute state of perception I could never have been aware of it. But, as it was, I knew very well that Sunil was stretching out his arm towards me. Yet even though I was aware of the movement, at the instant when his fingers touched my bare hand I felt a violent shock. Involuntarily my right arm lifted in a gesture of protest and dismay. But my left hand did not move. It was as if it were paralysed and could not move.

Then, Sunil began stroking my hand, softly and rhythmically. He was now very close to me; I could feel the heat of his body more strongly. The strange pleasant untamed smell seemed all around me. I tried to move my hand, but I could not. Suddenly I understood the reason for the excitement that was rising in me, and I turned away my head so that Sunil should not see the expression of my face. Abruptly he stopped caressing my hand. An instant later I could feel his fingers unbuttoning the sleeve of the blouse I was wearing. Then I felt his hand begin to stroke my wrist. And as his palm moved up and down the length of my arm I began to tremble, and this trembling extended all over my body. Slowly I could feel Sunil's hand moving gently to my shoulders, and presently slide downwards until it reached my breast. I knew, then, a happiness so fierce that I could have cried out with the joy and pain of it. I made no more effort to consider resisting what I knew would be the very thing I had always longed for. I turned round my head and gazed up at the boy who was leaning over me. At that moment, very tenderly, with his eyes opened wide with awe as if he were performing some precious rite, Sunil bent down and kissed my lips. His mouth was wonderfully soft. Soon I could feel his tongue pressing and sliding against my teeth, and he gave a little cry of entreaty. Then I must have yielded, for his tongue was in my mouth, exploring and caressing. As if they were no part of my being, I now felt my arms clasp the boy's shoulders and draw him close to me.

I was no longer conscious of time. It was as if I had fainted for a while, because I seem to have forgotten the next few minutes. Dimly I knew that Sunil was undressing me. I was aware that he was stripping off his own clothes, but I remember nothing clearly until he stood naked in front of me. Then my excitement was immediate, for my senses and my heart joined together in wonder. Sunil's shoulders, I saw at once, were broad and strongly muscled. His deep chest narrowed down to a very small waist in the middle of which was the button of his flat belly, curled up like a knot in wood. His well-formed sinewy body was hairless and very dark, almost darker than soot. The skin of his thighs was so smooth that every part of their surface glittered like a mirror. He stood there, looking down at me, taut and quivering, his eyes fixed on mine. Around his neck he wore a thin silver chain. In silence we gazed at each other. Then he lay down beside me and put his arms round me.

All his shyness had now vanished. He was wholly dominant and absorbed in his passion. He was quivering with the intensity of his desire. He was fierce in his love-making. Yet there was a wonderful tenderness about him. When our two bodies joined together I knew that soon must come the ecstasy for which I had been waiting so long. I felt as if I were being lifted into the air and swung into the clouds. Only the joy of the present instant mattered—together with the litheness of Sunil's body, the softness of his skin and the burning of his virility inside me. And when the long moment of ecstasy came, I clutched the boy to me and held him pressed hard against me as if I would never let him go. But then it was all over, and I felt a delicious calm spreading all over me, and I thought of a ship that has travelled day after night across vast oceans, with bitter waves dashing violently against it, but now reaches harbour and glides across the tranquil waters to security.

Presently, I was lying there quietly on the grassy bank. Sunil's arms were around my waist and his head was resting between my breasts. There was a proud expression on his face. I wondered if this was because he had been so ardent and was proud of his virility. But then I noticed there were tears shining in his eyes, and I knew they must be tears of happiness. I now observed that from the silver chain around his neck there hung a very small cross. I took the cross in my hand and held it up enquiringly. Sunil smiled and nodded his head.

'Mission School,' he muttered, and wrinkled his nose in distaste. Then he raised himself and kissed the skin of my shoulders and then my mouth, and soon he was making love to me again.

———————◆◆◆◆————————

As we rode home that evening, my whole body seemed to glow with happiness. We were silent. For our hearts and bodies had joined together, and, at present, there was no need for any further communication.

10

I enjoyed the sherry party at the Resident's house. People may say that Olivia Maxwell is conceited and overbearing; I have always found her full of affability. And she is a charming hostess. Gerald Maxwell was as stiff as ever. I'm afraid the poor man simply cannot make himself natural or pleasant. But I enjoyed the occasion. I was only sorry that Anne looked so pale and listless. I suppose she was annoyed that it had meant she could not go out riding that afternoon.

At dinner, Anne refused the meat course.

'Take just a little,' I urged.

'No, thank you, Margaret,' Anne replied. 'I'm not hungry.'

'I thought you were looking a bit unwell this evening,' Tom told her. 'And yesterday evening too, now I come to think of it.'

'I have a headache,' Anne answered.

'Then you should never have gone to the party,' I told her.

Anne turned towards Tom. 'You wanted me to,' she said to him.

Tom frowned. 'I'd rather you stayed at home than sat in a corner hardly talking to anyone,' he replied.

Tom had not spoken at all sharply, but for some reason Anne was immediately upset.

'What had I got to talk to all those people about?' she cried out. 'They're simply not interested in the things that interest me. Not one little bit.'

'What you mean is that *you're* not interested in the things that interest *them*,' I told Anne.

'How do you know I'm not?' Anne asked.

'I can see it with my own eyes,' I answered. 'Their conversation bores you, and sometimes you can't be bothered to disguise your boredom.'

'What do you expect me to do?' Anne replied.

'Ask them questions,' I told her. 'Everyone likes to talk about themselves, so ask them about their servants or their horses or their children.'

Anne raised her fair head and stared at me with her wide blue eyes. At that moment, in her undisguised indignation, I must admit that she looked extremely pretty.

'But I don't care about their children,' Anne answered. 'I don't *know* their children, so why should I be interested in them?'

Tom laughed. 'You're too honest,' he said. 'You're too honest by far. That's your trouble. All the same, you must try to make an effort to make friends with some of the wives of the officers.'

As Tom spoke, Anne blushed, and I could not understand why.

'You must try to enter into the life we lead out here,' Tom continued. 'Why not come and watch the polo match tomorrow?'

'Or would it interfere once again with your afternoon ride?' I asked her.

Anne did not answer me. She turned to Kumar, who was handing round a dish of strawberries.

'Kumar,' Anne said, 'will you please tell Sunil that I won't be riding tomorrow?'

Kumar salaamed.

'Yes, Memsahib,' he answered.

<hr />

The sun shone brilliantly from a pale-blue sky. In the section reserved for Indians to the left of the grounds, the wonderful colours of the women's saris glittered with brilliance. Anne and I were sitting in the grandstand, surrounded by the wives of

Tom's officers. The score of the chukka was even—with five minutes to go.

Marjorie Russell was placed on the other side of me. She looked more buxom than ever, almost inclined to stoutness. I noticed that her eyes were more often fixed on the Rajah than on her husband.

'The Rajah rides remarkably well,' she murmured, as if in apology for her concentrated gaze. 'I'll say that for him.'

Susan Phillips was sitting on the other side of Anne. She too had been watching the Rajah eagerly, noting each movement he made. She was devoted to riding and to horses, and, like so many women who spend half their lives in the saddle, she had come to look rather like a horse herself, with her lean face, her long nose and wide nostrils. Susan overheard Marjorie's remark about the Rajah and turned to Anne.

'I'm sure Anne agrees,' Susan said. 'Don't you, Anne?'

'After all,' Marjorie chipped in, 'he's quite a friend of yours, isn't he? I'm told you went to tea with him at the palace.'

'I think both Tom and the Rajah ride excellently,' Anne replied.

Marjorie laughed. '*There's* a tactful answer for you!' she said.

Joan Rigg, a small perky little woman who always wore too much powder on her face, now leaned forward to Anne.

'The Rajah's got a whole string of polo ponies,' Joan told her. 'So he can ruin as many as he likes.'

'Just look at him now,' Susan cried out.

Tom had got the ball and was moving towards the goal. The Rajah spurred his pony and caught up with Tom. The two ponies were now galloping side by side. Out of the corner of my eye I could see that Marjorie's mouth was working with excitement. The Rajah was now passing Tom. Then I saw him pull round his pony to cut Tom off. Suddenly the Rajah's pony fell. But Tom had already swerved away, and he galloped on to score a goal. The Rajah picked himself up off the ground. He was quivering with rage. Two Indian syces rushed up and pulled the pony to its feet.

'Take the pony and lock it up in the stables,' the Rajah muttered to them in Tamil.

'Poor pony,' Marjorie murmured.

'But it doesn't seem lame,' Anne said.

'Of course I forgot, you don't speak Tamil,' Marjorie replied. 'Well, I must tell you that the dear Rajah has told his two syces to take the pony to the stables and he'll probably have it shot.'

There was applause as Tom rode past the grandstand.

'Well, we won,' Tom said when he joined Anne and me at the club afterwards. 'But it was a close thing.' His face was flushed, and I could see that he had already had a drink or two. But for once I did not mind, for I felt that he had deserved it.

'Is it true?' Anne asked him.

'Is what true?' Tom enquired.

'That the Rajah might have his pony destroyed,' Anne said.

'He can afford to,' Tom answered. 'He's got two dozen more.'

'Can't you stop it?' Anne asked.

'How can I stop it? The pony belongs to him,' Tom pointed out. 'If he wants to have it shot, how can I interfere?'

Marjorie Russell had come up to us, drink in hand. She turned to Anne. 'I should have thought that *you* were the one to stop him,' Marjorie told Anne. 'After all, this afternoon it was only you that he wanted to impress.'

'What nonsense!' Anne exclaimed.

'Couldn't you see him staring at you whenever he got the chance?' Marjorie asked.

Tom forced himself to smile.

'Or perhaps he was staring at Marjorie's coat,' Tom said, turning to her. 'That yellow silk is really superb.'

Marjorie simpered. 'Thank you,' she replied, gazing up at Tom coyly. Then she drifted away towards the bar.

That evening there was a Mess Night, so Anne and I dined alone. After dinner, when we had moved into the drawing-room I decided that I must speak to Anne seriously. I was aware that for the past two days she had seemed rather seedy; I knew that she was unusually nervous and highly strung, so I spoke to her gently.

'Anne, my dear,' I began slowly and rather tentatively, 'I hope you know how pleased I am to have such a delightful and attractive sister-in-law. I'm so grateful to have a companion at last. I don't mind telling you that before you came, when Tom was away at the barracks, I found it very lonely here in this large house. So from every point of view I am glad you have arrived out here.'

Anne closed the book of poetry which she had taken up. 'Thank you,' she replied.

I put down my knitting. I know that the clicking of my needles annoys Tom whenever we are talking together, so I dare say it worries Anne as well.

'Please don't think I'm criticising you in any way,' I said. 'But I want you to understand the realities of living up here on this hill-station. Almost all the regimental wives have got far more servants than they need. Their head bearer generally runs the household for them. So they have plenty of time to themselves, and very little to do except gossip. They're not malicious. They don't intend to cause any harm. But chattering about each other's private affairs has become a habit with them. I tell you this so that you should understand the various remarks which were made today at the polo match, and later in the club. I'm referring to the remarks made about yourself and the Rajah. Now I'm perfectly aware that nothing in the slightest degree improper has gone on between the two of you. However, somehow the news that you had tea alone with the Rajah at the palace has spread about and has become common knowledge. Hence those rather catty comments that were made today. It's in no way your fault. But I think that for your own sake and for Tom's sake you ought to be very careful.'

As I spoke, Anne had begun to blush. 'Very well,' she answered. 'Let me tell you that I shall never go to the palace again. Never.'

'That's not quite what I meant,' I explained to her quietly.

'I think it better that you should never go again to the palace *alone* even if you're promised that the Ranee will be there. But obviously, if Tom is invited to the palace you must accompany him.'

'But I won't,' Anne replied. 'I've just told you. I intend never to visit the palace again.'

A log had fallen from the fire into the grate. I got up and replaced it with the tongs. Then I went back to my chair and looked towards Anne. She was glaring at me.

'I'm afraid I've made you angry,' I said to her. 'I didn't mean to.'

'I'm not angry,' Anne answered. 'All I've done is to tell you that I won't go to the palace again.'

'That will be for Tom to decide,' I told her.

'No!' Anne cried suddenly. 'It won't be for Tom to decide. You both of you try to treat me as a child. In fact you try and *make* me into a child. But I'm not a child. Not any longer. So I won't be dealt with as if I were a child. Now do you understand?'

'I understand perfectly well,' I answered. 'But you will be dealt with as Tom sees fit.'

Anne rose from her chair. For a moment she stared at me in silence, tense and shaking.

'But I won't!' Anne cried out. 'I'll be treated as a grown-up human being.'

'When you married Tom,' I reminded her, 'you promised that you would love him and obey him.'

'What archaic nonsense!' Anne exclaimed. 'As if anyone at all educated believed in that rigmarole nowadays!'

' "That rigmarole," ' I told her, 'happens to be the creed in which all Christians believe.'

'Then I'm not a Christian,' Anne answered. She was now glaring at me in open defiance.

'You're tired,' I told her. 'Or you wouldn't say such a stupid thing.'

'Yes, I'm tired,' Anne answered. 'I'm tired of being treated like a child. I'm tired of being preached at.'

Anne moved swiftly towards the door and opened it.

'So now, if you'll excuse me, I will leave you,' she said. 'Good-night, Margaret.'

Anne closed the door behind her. But she did not go upstairs. I could hear her walking along the corridor to her little sitting-room. Then I heard the sound of a key turning in a lock.

II

As soon as I had turned the key in the lock, I began to feel ashamed of my fit of temper. After all, Margaret had been perfectly within her rights to warn me about the danger of gossip. And who was I to resent her warning? If ever the truth were uncovered, then in Margaret's eyes, in everyone's eyes, and in fact, I had broken one of the Commandments. I had sinned. I was guilty of a crime. I had committed adultery. The monstrousness and rashness of what I had done now struck me so forcefully that for a while I feared I would lose control of my senses. I was most horribly afraid. I had made love to one of my husband's servants. I had betrayed Tom's trust in me. And what did I know about Sunil? How could I tell that Sunil's first gesture of love had not been inspired by some obscure desire for revenge on his master or on the society to which he was forced to submit? What if Sunil were to boast of it to his friend Doshan? What if Doshan were to inform Kumar?

My head was swirling. I felt weak. I sat down at my desk. A faint light came from the embers of the fire. The curtains were only half-drawn. I stared out at the moon, shining down on the stableyard. I looked down at my left hand. I could still remember vividly the precise sensation I had felt when Sunil's fingers had touched my wrist. Suddenly an image of Sunil filled my mind: I could see his wide shoulders and his narrow waist and the firmness of his gleaming thighs. Odd images now slid into my vision. In garish tints I could see the village bazaar, close-packed with bullock carts and with Tamil women staggering under loads of firewood. The streets were crowded with

Indians of every age, their eyes all set in one direction. For they were staring at me. The picture faded. I now saw two ayahs gazing in at me through the window. The image was so real that I went to the window and peered out into the yard. But there was no one there. I drew the curtains. Now I could perceive a group of the officers' wives on the lawn of a long bungalow with their eyes fixed on me. Next I could see three officers leaning on the balcony of the club, each with a glass in his hand, each smoking a cheroot, with their eyes glaring accusingly straight at me. Then, once again, I saw Sunil standing as he had stood before me in the glade, naked and taut and expectant. I could feel his hand on my breast, and I could feel the fierceness of his embrace and the strength of his passion throbbing inside me, and, presently, the tenderness of his kisses on my flesh. As I now envisaged his smile and the clearness of his eyes, I realised that there was no guile about Sunil. The passion which had inflamed him had been spontaneous and natural. As I sat there, considering Sunil in every aspect, I discovered with a stab of anguish that I was in love with him. I tried to struggle against this realisation, but it was useless. I began to think over each afternoon that I had gone out riding with Sunil. Then, at last, I saw the truth. When I rehearsed our previous rides together through the forest I could now remember small incidents and details of Sunil's attitude. I could recollect odd gestures and behaviour which at the time I had neglected or had not bothered to understand. But now, as small incidents came back into my mind, I could perceive that they amounted to a complete picture. They combined to convince me that Sunil in his turn was in love with me.

While I sat motionless at the desk, lines of poetry began to form in my mind. I looked at the clock on the mantelpiece. I knew that Tom would not be back for at least two hours. I rose and put a log on the fire. They I went back to my desk, and, knowing that the act of writing always had the power to make me forget my worries and distress, I began to work.

Adultery! The moon and stars permitted it.
  Adultery! I'm numbered with the thieves.
Adultery, and it was I committed it
  I hear it in the whisper of the leaves.
The servants creep about, their looks are sidelong
  They seem to spy on everything I do,
And sense that one who has not been a bride long
  Already to their master is untrue.

Women at parties seem about to utter,
  See me and stop; While underneath the stars
Men on verandahs lower their tones and mutter
  And soon we'll be the talk of the bazaars.
Let them go on with their malicious chatter
Our love, our sacred love alone will matter.

12

I enjoyed the Mess Night less than usual—perhaps because I was worried about Anne's health. If she is unwell in the bracing climate of Telecamund, how will she be able to endure the stifling heat of the plains.

Because I was worried, I drank far too much, and I can scarcely remember riding Jupiter back followed by Doshan on the roan mare. However, as we approached the house, I sobered up a little. There were no lights in the upper windows, so both Anne and Margaret had gone to bed and to sleep. I dismounted, threw the reins to Doshan, greeted the night-watchman and walked unsteadily into the house. I picked up the lamp which was burning in the hall. Then I hesitated. Anne was asleep, and I decided that I was still too drunk to wake her. I would sleep in my dressing-room. In that case, I argued with myself, there was no reason why I should not have a night-cap before turning in. I went into the dining-room and poured my-self a large whisky from the decanter on the sideboard. As I drank, I made another decision. I determined to go and make an inspection of Anne's sitting-room. There was always a chance that I might discover a poem. I was so pleased with this idea that I took a second drink to celebrate. Then I walked out of the room with the lamp in one hand and yet another drink in the other. The sitting-room door was half open. I went in and kicked the door shut behind me. I put down the lamp on the desk. I took the key out of the bronze jar. I unlocked the drawer and pulled it open. There were several sheets of blank paper. I began turning them over one by one. Presently I came to a sheet with writing on it. I took it out of the desk and held it up to the lamp. My eyesight was blurred and at first I could not read. The lines jumped and flickered before my eyes. It was some time before I could even decipher the very first line. It was longer still before I had finished reading the poem. I put down the sheet of paper. I took a long gulp of my drink. Then I decided to go through the poem again, trying to concentrate on the meaning which lay behind each hideous line of betrayal. I was sick from disgust and anger. For an instant I contemplated rushing upstairs and waking Anne. Then I determined that whatever I did I must first follow my original plan: I must steel myself to read the poem line by line, however painful it might be. I took up the sheet of paper. But my mind was confused by the anguish of my thoughts, and as I now read, pictures quite different from the lines of the poem were illuminated in my brain with a ghastly horror.

As I drank, I could see the palace glittering in the moonlight.

'I'm numbered with the thieves,' The line churned round in my brain. Suddenly a picture of the 'English room' was imprinted on my mind, and I saw the Rajah, dressed in a tight-fitting gold tunic and light blue trousers, walking up and down the room. His drawn-back lips bared his teeth, which gave a sinister expression to his face. He stopped in the middle of the room and smiled. I could not see the person to whom he was smiling, but I knew instinctively it was Anne, so I was not surprised when she advanced from the far end of the room. Then the Rajah turned away from her and moved towards a painting of an old man which was hanging low on the wall. He raised his finger and pointed it towards the man's left eye in the portrait. I now perceived that within the eye was a small almost invisible circle which seemed to be made of metal. As the Rajah's finger reached forward and pressed against it, I realised that it was a secret button. In the wall to the right of him a panel slid aside. It was a hidden door. Anne hesitated, then walked through the opening. The Rajah followed her.

In my drunken haze, I could now see into the room. It was decorated in a lurid oriental style. There were no windows. The light came from a lamp on a table beside a large bed covered with white satin which was placed beneath a scarlet canopy that flowed down from the ceiling. The Rajah went to a lacquered tray and poured out a cloudy liquid into two goblets. 'I'm numbered with the thieves.' The line still echoed in my head. I was aware that I was now dreaming although I was partly awake. But I could not shake off the terrible nightmare. Perhaps I was reaching a condition close to delirium. The Rajah raised his goblet first and drank. Then Anne raised her glass, tilted back her head and finished her drink. Immediately Anne changed. Her whole body became weak, almost torpid. Her lips parted in a sensual smile as she gazed at him with dilated blue eyes. The Rajah smiled once again. Then he went across and kissed her. When his lips touched her skin, Anne's arms encircled his neck. Presently he took her hand and led her towards the bed. Obediently Anne lay down. Presently he drew away from her.

For a while the Rajah stood gazing at Anne, stretched out on the white satin. Then he stooped down and began to unfasten her clothes. Anne made no protest. She lay there limp and inert while he pulled off her clothing until she was naked. For a second he leaned over her and cupped her breasts with his hands. Then be began to unbutton his gold tunic and to rip off his clothes until he, too, was naked. His body was obscene in its strength. He glanced down at Anne's slim form lying on the bed. Then he crossed to a long cupboard and slid open the door. Hanging in the cupboard were rows of whips and strange instruments of torture. Anne was still lying spread out on the bed. She was staring at the cupboard with an expressionless face. 'And it was I committed it.' The line was there as a proof of the scene I was witnessing.

In disgust I wrenched round my head in order to escape, and at that moment the revolting delusion left me, and I was once more standing alone in Anne's sitting-room. I now was filled with an overwhelming disgust at myself, for I knew that the visions I had seen had been produced by my own imagination and revealed a sadistic part of my nature that I had always tried to suppress. I felt violently sick. I moved towards the window because I was afraid I would vomit. I pulled it open. The clean night air swept cold against my face. I do not know how long I stood there, trembling with abhorrence at what my mind had conjured up. The nausea had now gone. I finished my drink in a gulp and managed not to retch. I put the poem back in the desk, locked the door and put the key in the jar. Then I left the room with the lamp in my hand and clambered up the stairs to our bedroom.

Anne was asleep in bed. Strands of her pale hair lay on the pillow. Quietly I put the lamp on the bedside table and stood looking down at her. She was breathing softly and steadily. With her unlined face, her smooth skin and her gentle features she looked like a young child. Flowing through my whole being I felt a wonderful tenderness towards her as I remembered that she was young enough to be my daughter and as I recollected how much I loved her. Then the line came lurching back into my head. 'I'm numbered with the thieves.' Once again my heart was pierced by doubt. But what proof had I got? None. The man whom I had sent to watch the palace had reported that Anne had never been anywhere near the grounds since the afternoon she had had tea alone with the Rajah. Surely, a young girl who was trying out her hand at poetry could write a sonnet about adultery without it being a reference to her own conduct? Surely, it was I who was guilty for my suspiciousness and my vile imaginings? By the light of the lamp I watched Anne's face and knew that it was the face of an innocent child.

As I stood like a sentinel beside the bed, Anne woke up. She stared up at me without recognition as she swam to the surface of consciousness. Then she saw who I was and, for a second, her face was contorted by an odd spasm of fear. A moment later the convulsion had vanished and she smiled up at me drowsily. But in that second I had glimpsed an expression which I was almost certain was a betrayal of guilt; I felt nearly sure of it.

Anne glanced at the clock on the bedside table.

'You're back late,' she murmured.

'I am indeed,' I answered.

'Why do you keep staring at me?'

'I was just wondering,' I replied.

'What were you wondering?'

I hesitated. I did not want to reveal my distrust to Anne, yet I wanted to probe into her state of mind.

'I was wondering how well I know you,' I replied.

Suddenly Anne flinched as if I had raised my hand to strike her.

'Why should you have such a thought?' she asked. 'You haven't been worrying yourself about the Rajah again?'

'No,' I answered. 'Is there any reason why I should?'

'None,' Anne answered promptly and vigorously. 'In fact, in the morning, I'm sure Margaret will tell you of my decision.'

'What decision?'

'After dinner this evening Margaret told me that there'd been some gossip about the Rajah and myself,' Anne said. 'So I've decided never to visit the palace again.'

'But I presume that you'll accompany me if we're both invited?'

'No,' Anne answered. 'I won't. I won't ever go to the palace again. I dislike him and all that he stands for.'

'Yet only a few weeks ago you told me that you found him amusing,' I pointed out. 'What could have happened to make you change your mind so rapidly?'

I saw the blood rising from Anne's neck and spreading over her face.

'I never found malicious gossip amusing,' Anne replied. 'Particularly when I'm the subject of it.'

'But you've never seen the man since the day you had tea alone with him, have you?' I asked.

Anne gazed at me with her large eyes. 'No', she answered calmly. 'I've never seen him since that day, and I never intend to see him again.'

'That's going to make our lives a little complicated,' I told her.

'Don't you see that it's the only way to put an end to all the petty gossip?'

Anne's attitude had been so indignant throughout our conversation that once again I found my suspicions were being melted away. I bent down and kissed the skin of her forehead.

Anne lifted her hand and stroked the side of my bristly cheek. Her eyelids had now begun to close.

'You're tired,' she murmured.

I smiled. 'So are you,' I replied. 'I think I'll sleep in the dressing-room for tonight, or what's left of it.'

'Yes,' Anne said. 'Perhaps you should.'

Once again I kissed her. Then I picked up the lamp, and fairly steadily I crossed to the door which led to my dressing-room.

◂•••▸

When I left the house in the morning Anne was still asleep, and I did not wake her. I was surprised to find that I had no headache, and my bewildered musings during the night now seemed no more than part of an unpleasant nightmare. I knew perfectly well that Anne had not made a secret visit to the palace. I was certain that she was innocent. My suspicions had only been formed because she had chosen to write a romantic poem about adultery. There was no more to it than that.

Lying on my desk in my office in the barracks there was a letter from Headquarters announcing that the Commander-in-Chief was coming to visit us.

Presently I rode out on to the parade-ground. As usual, the regiment was drawn up in two ranks. Captain Rigg was taking the parade. One of my officers stood in front of each company. As I appeared, followed by Poole, my Adjutant, Rigg gave his command in a loud bellow.

'Second battalion,' he roared out. 'Atten—shun!'

Then he walked smartly towards me and saluted me with his sword.

'All present and correct, sir,' he called out crisply. 'Seven hundred and ten on parade.'

'Thank you, Captain Rigg,' I said. 'Stand them at ease.'

'Stand at—ease!' Rigg shouted. 'Stand easy!'

I spoke in Tamil. I am fortunate that my voice is clear and carries without effort across a parade-ground.

'Now then,' I began. 'I'll make no inspection this morning.

But there'll be a full inspection each morning from now on. The Commander-in-Chief is doing our regiment the honour of paying us a visit shortly. I want our regiment to be the best turned-out and the best drilled of any regiment he's inspected on his tour . . . Captain Rigg!'

'Sir!'

'Captain Rigg—carry on.'

Rigg saluted, made an about-turn, marched back to his original position, and faced the regiment.

'Battalion!' he bawled out. 'Atten—shun! Slope—arms!'

I left the parade-ground followed by the Adjutant. Later in the morning, we made a tour of the barracks, taking note of all that had to be done before the great man's visit. As always when one searches for it, we found hundreds of things that needed attention. I felt content and happy. As I made my round of inspection, I remembered that it was time to look at our stables up at the house, for Kumar had told me that Sunil had grown slack once again.

13

That morning I awoke late. Tom had already left for the barracks, and when I went downstairs I discovered that Margaret had been driven in the carriage to a committee meeting. I went into my sitting-room. I decided to re-read my poem. I unlocked the drawer and pulled it open. I had taken to hiding any poem I wrote between other sheets of paper in case anyone should find the key of the drawer, though the eventuality was most unlikely, so I now began turning over the sheets of blank paper. To my surprise I found the poem below the fourth page. I was almost certain that I had hidden it further down—perhaps beneath the tenth sheet. I closed the drawer again and sat down at my desk and wondered. Both the bearers and the ayahs could read English. Could one of them be spying on me? What if Margaret or Tom had found the key and had read the poem? Could this explain an odd phrase or two that Tom used when he had awakened me the previous night? Or had his manner seemed odd to me merely because he had drunk too much? Probably the latter. Even so, I decided that I would never write down a poem again. I would compose it in my head and keep it in my head. I only compose a sonnet for my own satisfaction, so what difference does it make?

As I sat at my desk, vaguely staring out of the window, Sunil crossed the yard. He saw me. For an instant he stopped and slightly inclined his head in the direction of the gate of the compound. Then he moved on. I understood the meaning of his gesture: he wanted me to go out riding with him that afternoon. I did not move. I gave no indication that I had observed his sign. He continued on his way and went out of sight. I tried to make up my mind what to do. I was still desperately uncertain. But even if I could persuade myself that the loyalty I owed to Tom should triumph over the love I felt for the boy whose wide eyes had gazed at me with a look of such entreaty, what action could I take? How could I avoid going out riding with Sunil without arousing suspicion? What excuse could I make? I could think of none. Therefore, surely, it was safer to continue with my rides. So I must go out with Sunil in the afternoon. I was now convinced that Sunil would keep my secret. So I must explain to him that I had lost my head. I must tell him that it was all my fault and my responsibility, that I was deeply fond of him and would do all I could to help him, but we must never make love to each other again. And I would try to make him understand the reasons that forced me to this decision.

⬥◆⬥

As we set out that afternoon, a light wind was shuddering in the tops of the fir-trees. We rode in silence, with Sunil, as usual, a few yards behind me. As we reached the wood, the wind dropped, and the air became sultry beneath the trees which seemed to exude heat. I tried to begin my explanation to Sunil, but the words would not come into my mind and I could not speak. Our horses were walking quietly along the track. Sunil drew level with me. He turned and gazed at me. I looked ahead; I still could not find words to speak. Sunil broke the silence.

'This afternoon too little air,' he said. 'Too much warm.'

'Yes, it is,' I agreed.

Sunil now spoke very softly.

'Memsahib,' he began.

I still kept my eyes fixed on the ground ahead.

'Memsahib,' Sunil continued in a quiet hoarse voice. 'For two days we have not been out riding together.'

'I know,' I answered.

'Memsahib, why-for not?'

'Because there were other things I simply had to do,' I replied.

For a while Sunil was silent. I glanced at him and saw that his face was surly, and this expression always made him look younger than ever.

'Is Memsahib angry?' he asked after a pause.

'No,' I replied.

'Not angry with me?'

'No,' I repeated.

'Please,' Sunil said. 'Please, Memsahib, could we stop—later?'

'No, Sunil,' I heard my voice say firmly.

'Is it because you are sorry?' Sunil asked. 'Are you sorry that you had love with an Indian servant?'

'That's not the reason,' I told him. 'Of course it's not.'

'Is it because of the Colonel Sahib?'

'Yes,' I answered. 'And he must never find out. Never. For both our sakes.'

'How could he find out?' Sunil asked. 'Will you tell him? Will I tell him? You must know that I will never tell anyone. I will keep it a secret until the day I die. So why-for you afraid of the Colonel Sahib?'

'He's my husband,' I said. 'It's wrong to deceive him.'

'What is the best?' Sunil said. 'To deceive him or tell him the truth?'

'What we did was wrong,' I stated obstinately.

'Why wrong?' Sunil demanded. 'Is it wrong that I had love with you? When I have loved you from the day we first go riding together? When I would kill myself for you? When you are she who I love most in all world? If you are loving me, is it wrong that you should have love with me? Or do you not love me? Or are you ashamed for what you did because my skin is black?'

'No,' I cried out. 'You musn't say that, Sunil.'

'Or was it because it please you to make me in love you even more than I am before?' Sunil asked. 'Or do you like me just as a servant-boy—one that you could have love with and forget about?'

'You know that's not the truth,' I told him.

'Then why-for?'

'Because I'm afraid,' I answered. 'Because I want to be loyal to my husband.'

'Does loyal mean to be true and to honour and to love a person?' Sunil asked.

I suppose he was quoting some definition he had learned at the mission school.

'Yes,' I replied.

'I think you do love me,' Sunil said. 'I think your heart is loving me even though you are afraid. So you must be loyal to *me*—because I love you.'

I was silent. Our horses which had been walking very slowly now came to a halt.

'We are alone here,' Sunil said. 'No one is in this place. Please, Memsahib. All the last three nights I am thinking of you. And I need—I need you too much. Please let us rest here.'

I shook my head. Sunil bit his lip and was silent again. Suddenly the idea came into my mind that I might ride down to the lake to visit Rodney Meadows. At least it would break the strain that now existed between Sunil and myself. But our relationship had grown so tense that its nature might be visible to an outsider, and I believed that Rodney had a sharp intuition. Moreover, my conversation with Sunil had upset me. At a moment when Sunil suspected that the reason I would not make love to him again was because of the colour of his skin and because he was a servant, it would be unwise to enter a place where I would be invited to sit on the verandah while Sunil would be taken to the servants' quarters. However, the tension between us was hard to bear; I could not endure it much longer. Our horses were walking side by side along the track, and we were still silent. But it was as if our silence were in itself a form of conversation. I became very aware of Sunil's longing for me and of his bitterness that I would not stop and make love to him. In the surliness of Sunil's expression was now mixed an air of bewildered sadness, which hurt me. I urged Cara into a canter. I could hear that Sunil was following me. Though I was worried, I was still in control. I forced myself to become aware of the wood and of the interlacing branches above my head in which the crows were cawing monotonously. We came to the part of the track that was strewn with boulders; I reined in. Our two horses walked quietly. Presently, Sunil drew level with me once more.

'We stop some place,' Sunil whispered.

'No,' I answered.

A few minutes later we reached the little glade which was dappled with sunshine.

'We stop here,' Sunil said.

I shook my head. When we had reached the middle of the glade, Sunil reined in his horse and jumped down. A second later Cara came to a halt, but I made her walk on. I left the glade, with its blue and yellow wildflowers and springy turf. I glanced back and saw that Sunil had tethered his horse to a tree. But I did not stop. I rode onwards. I came to a fork in the track. I was afraid that the turning to the left might lead down to the lake, and I did not wish to pass Rodney's house, so I took the path to the right, which led through crimson rhododendron trees and tall cedars. The ground was covered with pale-blue flowers. Presently the wood grew thicker. I was now riding through a tunnel of dense foliage. The forest seemed to be pressing in on me. Cara was ambling along slowly. The air was fetid. The silence was so complete that I gave a start when a parrot screeched overhead. I felt forlorn. At that moment I believed I had little in life I could look forward to. I lowered my head in despair. My hands now lay slackly on the saddle. Presently Cara came to a halt, and for a while stood still. Then she gave a gentle snuffle and slowly turned around in the track and began to move in the direction of home. I made no attempt to stop her. Such was the intensity of my despair that I did not care what would happen. Nothing could be worse than my present anguish of spirit. Soon I came out of the dark wood and into the glade. Sunil was lying on the bank of grass which was still dappled by sunshine. He was naked except for his breeches. As I appeared, he sprang to his feet and rushed across to me. Cara stopped. Sunil cupped his hands for me to dismount. I hesitated. I could not stop myself staring at this young boy who stood gazing up at me. He was the most beautiful human being I had ever seen. But it was not only his physical charm which attracted me to him. He seemed to exude some force which was at once sweet and gentle and at the same time passionately sensual.

In silence I dismounted; in silence Sunil went to tether my horse. Far away in the distance I could hear the sound of goat-bells. Sunil came back to me slowly. He put his arms around me. Then, he kissed my lips while his hands moved lightly over my body. I could feel that I was trembling. Our mouths joined together. Sunil's fingers now began to undo the buttons of my riding-habit. He slipped his hand inside my blouse and began to feel my breasts. As he touched my body, I experienced a sense of respite from pain and a consolation of spirit. So wonderful was the entrancement which now invaded me that I believe that even if I had known Tom was approaching the glade, I could not have resisted Sunil's importuning caresses, nor the passion of his embrace. With shaking hands I helped him take off my clothes. Then, in a frenzy of impatience, he pulled off his breeches. Once again he stood before me naked. For a moment we stood facing each other. I felt his body quivering when he took me in his arms and led me to the bank of grass and made me lie down. He crouched beside me and began to kiss my forehead and my cheeks. I felt myself overwhelmed by a delicious joy. I still could remember my resolution never to make love to Sunil again. But this decision on my part now seemed to me an act of treachery for which I must show atonement—even though I had not revealed to him all the thoughts that were in my mind. Somehow I must show Sunil how intensely I loved him. I must prove to him that in our love we were equals and that no thought of his colour or caste in any way disturbed me. To do this I must be as flagrant in my passion as he was. So I raised myself and began kissing him. I kissed him from his throat to the skin stretched tight over his chest, sliding my mouth over the flatness of his stomach until I reached his groin. Then I pressed my face against his burning skin. I could feel him throb against my lips. With a wrench he pulled away from me. He grasped my shoulders and forced them against the grass. Violently he pressed down on me. Yet there was no pain as he thrust into me and our bodies were joined. Soon, I reached the ecstasy that was now more glorious than anything I had ever experienced. I could feel his whole body flooding into me in torrents of passion. And, afterwards, as we lay clasped together with our limbs entwined, I felt that I belonged to him and would belong to him forever.

In the glade it was very quiet. I could hear a lark singing and the sound of our horses cropping contentedly. Now and then a monkey would ruffle the leaves of the branches above us. Sunil spoke in a hoarse whisper.

'I love you,' he said. 'I love you too much. Yen anbé. My own darling.'

I could not remember the words I spoke as I covered his face with kisses; nor can I now remember how long we lay there on our carpet of green. Vaguely I was aware of monkeys scampering in the tall darkening trees and of a squirrel peering out at us from the dense foliage and of the sun's declining rays. And as I lay there in a haze of contentment and joy, gradually, and it seemed without any effort, lines of a poem came into my head.

> Now is my heart on fire, which once was chilled,
> Now are our bodies one which once were two,
> For you are part of me and I of you.

Oh deep strong calm when turbulence is stilled,
In this sweet union which God has willed.
  Come closer, rest, I tremble through and through,
  All you can want of me I gladly do,
Now is the purpose of our lives fulfilled.

Is He not good, God who such rapture gives?
  Such overflowing ecstacy of joy.
Touch, let me touch your warm enticing skin
That I may know my lover breathes and lives.
  My own, my darling sunkiss'd supple boy
If this is sinful, what is wrong with sin?

————◆••◆————

'Why is Memsahib silent?' Sunil asked as we rode home.

I laughed. I felt light-headed with happiness.

'Each time you call me "Memsahib",' I said, 'it makes me feel at least twenty years older than you. But in fact I'm only two years older. So you must call me by my name.'

'Anne,' Sunil began tentatively, 'Anne, something on our ride back has been a worry to you. Are you sorry?'

'Heavens, no,' I answered. 'I'm happy. Very happy.'

'Then why-for is Memsahib—why-for is Anne worried?'

'Because I'm afraid they might find out.'

'Never!' Sunil cried.

'When I'm with you and they're around I must be careful how I look at you,' I told him. 'Even a glance might give us away. You see, I know they're watching me.'

Solemnly, Sunil waggled his head in assent.

'When others are present,' he said, 'I promise I will never even let my eyes move towards you. For if the Colonel Sahib knew, he would have me whipped and sent away. And if the Rajah found out, then he would have me killed.'

'The Rajah? I asked in surprise.

'He would be jealous,' Sunil told me. 'And he would be mad in his anger.'

'Why do you say that?' I enquired.

'Doshan, the head syce, is my friend,' Sunil explained. 'He told me how the Rajah looked at you when you go to see the polo. Other people have also said he love you very much.'

'I don't think so.' I muttered.

'Yes,' Sunil answered. 'He love you too much. He want you. And if he found out—if he found out that I, Sunil, a low-caste servant, was your lover, then he would have me killed.'

'No,' I protested. 'I can't believe you. It's not possible.'

'It is the truth I am telling you,' Sunil replied. 'His anger is very great, and he has much power.'

'Perhaps . . .' I began, when Sunil interrupted.

'But I tell you some things,' he said. 'We need not worry too much. I tell to you why. The Colonel Sahib will not think you will let me make love to you because I am an Indian servant and because I am a boy. So he will never suspect me. And that is safe. Next thing is that the Rajah himself will not believe I will ever dare to make love to you. I am a Christian from the mission school. But to the Rajah I am still a Hindu. And he will find out about my family, for he has many spies in many places.'

'What can he find out?' I asked.

'To him it does not matter that my skin is black,' Sunil answered. 'But I am born of a low Hindu caste. He would not even look at me. To him I am not a boy nor a man. I am some-one who is not clean—like a leper. He would care no more of having me killed than if he killed a jackal on one of his shikars. So he will never think that you will let me even touch you. And he will never believe that you had let me make love to you.'

Sunil was gazing at me earnestly.

'When you have been here in Telacumund a time you will know that what I say is truth,' he continued. 'But in this wood we are safe I promise you. My ears are quick to hear. I will know if a man is near us. Yen anbé. Anne, do you promise you will ride tomorrow?'

'Yes,' I answered.

For a while we rode in silence. 'Sunil,' I said presently, speaking almost to myself, 'how long can we be together like this? How long can it last?'

'As long as the gods will,' Sunil answered.

'You say "gods", but there's a silver cross on the chain round your neck.'

Sunil smiled. 'I became a Christian to enter the mission school,' he explained. 'It was not difficult. All gods are much alike. My mother became Christian too. But her household gods are still in her home across the water. And she still makes her puja to them. She prays to them and makes them many sacrifices.'

'Is your father alive?' I asked.

'No,' Sunil told me. 'He died when I am a child, but I have one brother and two sisters.'

'Would your mother be angry if she knew about us?' I asked him.

Sunil laughed. But his voice when he spoke was bitter.

'No,' he answered, 'I might even gain merit in her eyes because I had been with a girl who was white.'

A swarm of monkeys hurried across the track. The sun was low in the sky. I would have to make an excuse for returning to the house a little late.

'If only life could be different,' Sunil cried out suddenly. 'If only my skin was white.'

'Would that help?' I asked.

'Then I would take you away,' Sunil said. 'But my skin is black. And as an Indian I am not even of good caste.'

'I read a Hindu proverb,' I told him. 'It says "Love heeds not caste, nor sleep a broken bed!" '

Sunil smiled. His face seemed to glow at the thought that had entered his mind. 'If you live with me,' he announced, 'the bed would never be broken, for I would make our bed very strong —because we would use it too much.'

I laughed and leaned across and stroked his cheek. Presently we approached the clearing that led down to the house.

'I will be thinking of you every moment of the rest of the day,' Sunil told me. 'In the night I will dream of you. And in the morning I will count the hours before we go riding together again.'

Then Sunil reined in his horse so that presently he was moving several yards behind me as the house came into view. I was still happy. Only dimly was I aware that behind my happiness lay guilt and a deep fear that I might have conceived a child with Sunil.

14

When I came back from the barracks that evening I found Margaret alone in Anne's sitting-room. She was standing by the desk. She held herself as erect as ever, but for the first time I noticed she was growing old.

'You've read the poem,' she said to me as I came in.

'Yes,' I replied. 'How do you know?'

'Last night I couldn't sleep,' Margaret explained. 'I heard you come back from the barracks. You went into the dining-room and then into Anne's sitting-room. I heard you open the door. And I guessed the reason. So I presume you took out the sonnet? I've also read it.'

There was silence. I was annoyed that Margaret had read the poem because I knew that she would consider it as an indictment of Anne.

'I came here as soon as I returned from the hospital committee to see if there was yet another poem,' Margaret continued, 'but there isn't. And to my surprise I discovered the poem I read this morning had gone. Anne must have burned it. Have you said anything to make her suspicious?'

'Perhaps,' I answered.

'After reading that sonnet, can there be much doubt left in our minds?'

'Poems are a work of the imagination,' I answered.

'In those lines, Anne appears to confess quite plainly that she's an adulteress.'

'She hasn't been again to the palace,' I told Margaret. 'I've had a definite report, and the man's reliable.'

As I spoke, an idea came into my mind. 'Margaret,' I began, 'do you think it's possible . . .'

'Do I think *what* is possible?' Margaret asked gently.

'Could the explanation be that in her *mind* Anne believes she has committed adultery?'

Margaret hesitated. 'You may be right,' she announced. 'Certainly that could be an explanation. *Perhaps* it's the truth.'

'You hate her, don't you?' I said to Margaret.

'No,' Margaret answered slowly. 'I don't hate her. That's just where you're mistaken. I would dislike anyone who made you unhappy, so at times I dislike Anne. But do you think I'm so stupid that I can't appreciate you're desperately in love with Anne, and that whatever happens you'll continue to love her? Do you think I don't understand that my position here has changed for good? Even if Anne were to leave you tomorrow, our relationship could never be the same again.'

'What do you mean by that remark?' I asked.

'When Anne first appeared on the scene,' Margaret explained, 'of course I was resentful. You and I had been happy alone together for many years, and I resented the intrusion of an outsider. So I tried to dislike Anne. I tried to persuade myself that she was a silly, obstinate girl, full of stupid ideas and conceit. But as the days have passed by, I've come to the conclusion that essentially Anne isn't like that at all. In fact, she is a rather shy and modest person who is very unsure of herself.'

Margaret's mouth had begun to slide in a nervous tic, and she turned away from me and looked down at the log burning on the fire which had just been lit.

'And this brings me to another point,' Margaret continued. 'If—and I only say if—you discover that Anne has been unfaithful to you, I want you to try to remain calm and to look ahead to the future. Supposing you make a ghastly scene and send Anne away from the house in disgrace, will that make you any happier? Of course not. You'd miss her most terribly, and you'd begin to resent my presence at the head of the table because it would not be Anne who was sitting there. So I want you to be reasonable. I want your common sense to triumph over your emotions. Supposing Anne has lost her head, then I want you to remember that, after all, she's a young girl, and it's perfectly possible. I would want you to be firm with her. But I would want you to be kind at the same time. I want no violent outburst. I want no reproaches flung at her face. You must say nothing that you would regret later, because, don't you see, you're going to have to go on living with her. Did Russell turn Marjorie out of the house when he found out that she had been having a flirtation with the Rajah? No. They probably had a fierce row, and that was the end of it. And they're still living together.'

I listened to Margaret carefully. I could appreciate her advice. But she was a woman. How could she possibly understand the complete disgust that would fill me if I knew Anne had been lying with another man? The very thought that her body which belonged to me had been used by another person would make me so sick that I doubt if I could ever touch her again. As I stared out of the window in silence, Anne approached the yard.

'Look!' I said to Margaret, and she came up to the window. Anne rode into the yard. For a moment I thought she was alone. But then Sunil appeared on the chestnut gelding about seven lengths behind.

'Kumar tells me that Sunil's half of the stables is filthy,' I told Margaret. 'The boy's getting slack again. I shall make an inspection tomorrow.'

Sunil slid off his horse, moved across to Anne, and helped her dismount. Anne did not even look at him. In silence she dismounted, handed the reins to Sunil and walked round the yard towards the front of the house. She was looking straight ahead of her. She did not even glance in the direction of her sitting-room.

'That was a bit odd,' I said to Margaret as we walked back to the drawing-room. 'No "thank you, Sunil". Not even a "good-night". By God! I wonder.'

'Impossible,' Margaret replied quietly.

'Let's hope so,' I said grimly. For the very thought revolted and horrified me.

'She wouldn't dare,' Margaret announced. 'Nor would Sunil. I'm absolutely sure of that. It's simply not possible. Anne would never even dream of such a thing, I promise you.'

Margaret spoke with such conviction that for a moment I decided my suspicion must be a result of my imagination. But Anne's behaviour had certainly been strange. She was always polite to servants—sometimes too polite. Yet she had not even said good-night to Sunil.

'You may be right,' I answered. 'But tomorrow could produce a method of making completely certain. It all depends on the state of the stables.'

After the morning parade I rode back to the house and went to inspect the stables. Doshan and Sunil were each of them responsible for looking after five of my horses. First, I walked along inspecting Doshan's section. The loose boxes were clean; the harness and saddles hanging from pegs on the walls were in good condition. But the curry-combs were broken, and I gave orders for new ones to be bought. I now moved on to Sunil's section.

Sunil was standing to attention in the corridor in front of the fifth loose box which contained the chestnut gelding I had seen him riding the previous day. I walked in. Doshan and Sunil followed me. The horse had been beautifully groomed. Its coat was smooth and glossy. I was aware that for some reason Kumar disliked young Sunil, and I began to think that Kumar had lied to me when he reported that the boy had been slacking. In the next box was White Star, one of my polo ponies. The pony whinnied as I approached. Immediately I could see that it's coat was in a bad state. I ran my hands over the pony's neck, then over its back and haunches. I turned to Sunil.

'When was this pony last groomed?' I asked.

'Early this morning, Sahib,' Sunil replied.

'Is that correct?' I asked Doshan.

He hesitated for an instant. 'Yes, Sahib,' he answered.

'Then it wasn't groomed properly,' I told him. 'Its coat is in a shocking mess.'

I kicked the straw with my feet.

'When was this straw last changed?' I asked.

'Yesterday, Sahib,' Sunil replied.

I picked up a wisp of straw and examined it. 'No, it wasn't,' I pointed out. 'This straw is at least four days old.'

I glanced towards Doshan. He was fond of Sunil, so I was not surprised that he looked worried and embarrassed. Moreover, as head syce, all the stables in our house were Doshan's responsibility. It was now obvious that Sunil had been shirking his work. I went out of the loose box to examine the bridles hanging in the corridor. I took up a bit and held it to the light.

'Look at this,' I said. 'This bridle has not been cleaned for ages. Just look at it, Sunil.'

'Sahib, I clean it yesterday,' Sunil muttered.

But I scarcely listened to him, for I was now examining a saddle which was in obviously bad condition. 'The leather is dirty, and dry to the point of cracking,' I told Sunil. 'You've got saddle-soap, I take it?'

'Yes, Sahib.'

'Then use it.'

I walked along the corridor, looking in at the other three horses and examining the saddles and bridles on my way. I was dismayed by the filth of the whole place.

'I'm aware that this is Sunil's section,' I told Doshan. 'But you're the head syce, so it's your business to see to it that Sunil does his work properly.'

'Yes, Sahib,' Doshan replied. 'I am sorry, Sahib.'

As I turned to Sunil, I saw a sudden flash of insolence in his eyes. Then it was gone.

'There's muck and dirt everywhere,' I told Sunil. 'The bridles are filthy. This section is a disgrace. I'm going to have you punished. You'd better go out into the yard and wait for Kumar.'

I never like to look on when one of my servants is being punished, but I realised that today must be an exception. I walked into Anne's sitting-room. She got up from her desk. I watched her face carefully. She looked pale, but I could detect no other sign of emotion.

'What's happening?' Anne asked.

I went to the window. Sunil was naked to the waist, facing the stableyard wall. His wrists had been tied to two rings about six feet high.

'I inspected the stables this morning,' I explained to Anne. 'Sunil's section was disgusting. He's become thoroughly lazy, so he's going to be punished.'

As I spoke Kumar came into the yard. He was carrying a whip which was about one inch thick at the butt and tapered down to a pencil point.

'Is a whipping going to make Sunil clean the stables any better?' Anne asked.

'I'm sure of it,' I answered.

'I doubt if you're right,' Anne said. 'And I must tell you that I'm surprised you should find Sunil lazy because each time I've been out riding with him I've happened to notice that Cara and his horse were impeccably well groomed.'

'Cara is looked after by Doshan,' I told Anne. 'The chestnut gelding was the only one of Sunil's five horses that had been cared for properly.'

Kumar had turned towards me as I stood at the open window, waiting for me to give the word for him to begin.

'You're the master of the house,' Anne said, 'as I am constantly reminded. So you will do what you please. And I know that you'll take little notice of my opinion. But I consider that to whip a boy like Sunil is barbaric and brutal.'

Anne was trembling with the intensity of her defiance. I now measured the effect of each word I spoke.

'You must remember that I know these people,' I said. 'But, of course, if Sunil is a special friend of yours, if he's one of your pet favourites, I suppose I had better call off his punishment.'

I paused. I was watching Anne closely. Her face was expressionless.

'Have you developed some romantic affection for Sunil?' I asked. 'Some schoolgirl passion?'

'No,' Anne answered coolly. 'Of course not. But I'd say that as a syce Sunil tries to do his work as well as he can. In fact, from the very first day you sent him out to accompany me on my ride, I've never had occasion to find fault with him.'

'That doesn't alter the fact that he is lazy,' I replied.

Anne's lofty attitude was beginning to annoy me. I nodded my head. Kumar raised his whip and slashed it across Sunil's back, leaving a red streak of blood. Anne turned away and sat in an armchair by the mantelpiece with her back to the window.

'I must admit it's horrible to watch,' I said.

'So is any unnecessary brutality,' Anne answered.

Kumar was now lashing the boy violently. Blood was oozing from the weals on Sunil's skin. I looked at Kumar. His face was distorted in a gloating leer. I could bear the spectacle no longer.

'Stop!' I cried out in a tone of command.

Reluctantly Kumar lowered the whip.

'That will be enough,' I called out.

Doshan hurried across the yard and untied Sunil's wrists. Sunil tried to walk, but he stumbled. Doshan helped him to the outhouse near the stables where they lived. I turned to Anne.

'I'm sorry,' I said to her. 'I've seldom watched a whipping before, and I must confess that I agree with you. It's unnecessarily brutal.'

Anne did not answer. I left the room. I poured myself a drink in the dining-room and went to see Margaret. She was reading a newspaper as I came in.

'You were right,' I told her. 'I watched Anne carefully. I was wrong. I'm absolutely sure she's completely innocent—so far as Sunil is concerned.'

'I thought as much,' Margaret replied. 'At least Anne knows something about the meaning and importance of caste out here. I took great care to "explain the form", as you put it, about *that* matter as soon as she arrived.'

I took a gulp of my drink. I felt a sense of weariness and despair creeping over me. I put down my glass and moved towards Margaret.

'What can I do?' I asked her quietly. 'Each time I manage to offend Anne, I know I'm only hurting myself. Margaret, what can I do?'

'Be firm,' Margaret answered. 'And wait. If my guess is correct, I think that Anne's little flirtation with the Rajah is finished. I was very angry with her at the time, I confess. I was really bitter. But now I intend to put it out of my mind and to forget. And you'd be wise to do the same.'

15

The day after Sunil had been whipped I made an excuse not to go out riding, and I observed that neither Tom nor Margaret seemed surprised. For some reason Margaret had been unusually gentle to me throughout the day.

The following afternoon I drove with Margaret down to the barracks to be present at the Commander-in-Chief's parade. As we entered the grandstand I was greeted by Marjorie Russell, who kept me talking for a while so that by the time we had climbed up to the rows of seats I was separated from Margaret.

Tom was standing beside the Commander-in-Chief at the saluting base. Behind them in a small enclosure were a cluster of Indian servants, among whom I noticed Belur and Doshan. The sun shone down from a cloudless sky. The flags were stirred by a slight breeze. The regimental band was playing loudly. I remembered the day when I had heard the strident chords of Mendelssohn's Wedding March. It seemed a very long time ago. I had been a different person on that occasion. One of Tom's officers marched smartly at the head of each company which was paraded in columns of four. As each company approached the flag, which marked the saluting base, the officer commanding the company would give the order, 'Eyes right' and he would come up to the salute with his sword. After the unit had passed the flag on the far side of the base, the officer would give the order, 'Eyes front', while the band continued to play the Regimental March. As each unit passed him, the Commander-in-Chief would raise his hand briskly and acknowledge the salute. He still looked young with his lean figure and grey moustache. His movements were alert, but his face was lined with weariness.

Marjorie Russell turned to me.

'The Rajah was invited to attend this afternoon,' she told me. 'But he sent his apologies and a message to say he was unwell. All the same, I do wish he'd been here to see this.'

'Why?' I asked.

'Because it should show him what natives can do when they're properly disciplined,' Marjorie replied. 'But then perhaps he wouldn't like it. You see, my dear, I'm sure he would prefer to take the salute himself.'

Marjorie paused while a sonorous voice cried out, 'Eyes right'. As they passed by us, the stamp of soldiers' feet could be heard above the sound of the band. Then came the command, 'Eyes front'. Marjorie turned back to me.

'You weren't at the polo match yesterday,' she stated.

'No,' I answered.

'The Rajah was riding a new pony,' Marjorie told me. 'They say the last one was put down, poor brute. The Rajah's almost as impetuous as your husband.'

Suddenly I could see the welts on Sunil's back, raw and bleeding. Horror filled my mind. The noise of the band seemed hideously loud and distorted. I began to sway. Vaguely I was aware that Marjorie was staring at me.

'You don't look well,' she said. 'You've gone quite ashen. Let me drive you home.'

I controlled myself. I rose from my seat. 'Thank you very much,' I mumbled. 'It's most kind of you. But I've got the carriage.'

I looked towards Margaret, who was deep in conversation with Susan Phillips in the front row.

'Could you be very kind and tell Margaret I've gone home?' I asked Marjorie. 'I'll send the carriage straight back for her.'

'Certainly, my dear,' Marjorie answered. 'But please do lie down when you get home. You look quite ill.''

On the way back in the carriage only one thought kept beating in my mind: 'I must see Sunil. I must see him.' When the carriage drove up under the porte-cochère I got out and watched it drive away. I entered the house and took off my hat. I went out into the stableyard. I looked around to make sure there was no one about. Then I moved towards the outhouse where Doshan and Sunil lived. Silently I approached the door which was shaded by a thick clump of firs. As I came close, suddenly a soft voice spoke from behind me.

'Good afternoon, Memsahib.'

I swung round. Kumar was standing in the shadow of the trees. As usual his narrow mouth was stretched into a smile.

'Good afternoon, Kumar,' I said. 'Is Doshan anywhere about? It was hot down at the barracks so I thought I might go for a ride to get some fresh air.'

Kumar's shoulders gave a slight twitch. He was still smiling, but his eyes were now examining me cautiously.

'Doshan is watching the parade,' he replied. 'Sunil is sick today, so he cannot do his work in the stables. But Sunil tell Doshan he will be able to go out with the Memsahib for the ride tomorrow.'

'Thank you, Kumar,' I said. Then I moved back towards the house.

———◆◆◆◆———

That next afternoon while Sunil and I rode through the forest I explained to him that I could not have risked going any further than I had done in trying to prevent Tom from having him whipped because I felt that Tom was already slightly suspicious of me.

Sunil's attitude surprised me.

'I had not done my work in the stables,' he said. 'I had groomed my own horse well and cleaned its harness because I wanted it to look smart when I went out riding with you. But when I came to grooming the other horses I had no heart for my work. For I would be thinking of you all the time. So I became lazy. The Colonel Sahib was right. I *was* lazy, so I must be whipped.'

At first I was a little dismayed by Sunil's fatalistic acceptance of what had happened—particularly since I could see that he still was in pain. Then, with a surge of gratitude, I realised that he had dismissed his whipping as if it were of small account in order to spare me embarrassment.

And now we were in the glade, and once again we had made love, and I was leaning against the trunk of a tree that rose from the soft grass, and Sunil was lying asleep on my lap. I gazed down at his back. The weals were still horribly raw. To my love for him was now added compassion. He was sleeping deeply. I longed to stroke his raven-black hair, but I did not wish to wake him. Presently the first few lines of a sonnet came slowly into my mind.

Now has the utmost cruelty been done!
 Oh, my own darling could I take your pain,
 And share it with you! Let the heavens rain
Healing upon my wounded lovely one.
See the spilt blood is drying in the sun.
 The great weals change to living flesh again,
 But your deep wound has not been made in vain,
Is this the way fulfilment has begun?

Sunil had begun to stir in his sleep. Then he stared up at me drowsily and smiled. I began to stroke his hair. Suddenly the smile left his face. He raised himself on one arm and listened intently. Then he put a finger to his lips to silence me and sprang to his feet.

'What is it?' I whispered.

But Sunil was now running swiftly across the glade. Without a sound he disappeared into the undergrowth. The tenseness of his expression had told me something was wrong. I rose in alarm. Hurriedly I began to put on my clothes. Faintly in the distance I could hear the rapid beat of a horse galloping. An instant later Sunil rushed back into the glade. His eyes were dilated, and he was trembling. For a moment he was so distraught he could not speak. He looked almost insane.

'It was the Rajah's man,' he managed at last to gasp out. 'It was Ashur, his secretary. Ashur, his spy. When I came towards him, he ran to his horse and he galloped away.'

With shaking hands Sunil seized his clothes and began to dress himself.

'He has seen us,' Sunil stammered out. 'I was asleep or I would have heard. He has been watching us, he has been spying on us. In an hour's time the Rajah will know. He will know the truth. In his anger he will send men to kill me.'

'But in the house,' I protested, 'surely you'll be safe in the house? In the compound how can anyone harm you?'

'Do you think the Rajah's men cannot enter the compound?' Sunil cried out. 'The walls are not high. With ropes they will climb them. He will find dacoits. He will pay men who are used to murder.'

'But, Sunil . . .' I began.

'Cannot you understand?' Sunil interrupted, his face twisted in desperation. 'Cannot you understand that in the Rajah's land there will be no place where I can hide. His spies are in every village. If I do not leave this country I will be killed like a dog. I told you this before. I told you. I had warned you. I must go. I must reach the sea to cross the water, and you must come with me.'

'But where, Sunil?' I asked him. 'Where?'

'Across the water to Ceylon to the village where is my home,' Sunil answered. 'There we will be safe—both of us. But we must go quick.'

I stared at him. I was so dazed that I scarcely understood what was happening.

'We must go,' Sunil repeated.

I could not answer. The thought of abandoning the place I called home dismayed me. How could I leave Tom and Margaret without a word? How could I escape from them like a thief and a deserter? Riding the horse that Tom had given me? Yet if I loved Sunil, what else could I do? And if I stayed and Sunil went off to Ceylon, might not the Rajah be tempted to tell Tom what had been discovered? I tried to force myself to remain calm. As I stood watching him, Sunil put on his tunic.

I began to see my predicament in a more detached perspective. If I now fled away from home like a coward I would never forgive myself. Certainly, I must leave Tom. That course now seemed inevitable. But I would leave him, if it were possible, with respect and dignity. Practical considerations also began to flood into my mind. How could I go away from the country with only the clothes I stood up in? I had no money with me. Sunil's family was poor. How could we live in Ceylon? If I had time to plan my departure I could take with me the pieces of jewellery that I owned, and Sunil could sell them for me. But how did I know that his mother would welcome me? Would she be pleased to greet a European woman who had run away from her husband and was penniless? I now saw the truth. I could not leave with Sunil immediately. That much had become clear to me. But somehow I must try to make Sunil understand my decision.

'Won't it be easier for them to follow two horses than one?' I asked.

'Yes,' Sunil answered. 'But you must still come with me.'

'I can't,' I said quietly. 'Not at this very moment.'

Sunil crossed over to me and gripped my hands. He was close to hysteria.

'If you do not come,' he cried out, his eyes glaring at me wildly, 'then I will stay here to be killed.'

'I must have time to think,' I told him. 'You must try to understand, Sunil.'

'To think,' Sunil replied. 'What is it that you can think? You love me, and I love you even more than my life. *That* is all you can think.'

As he spoke, I felt as if I had been living in a dream from which I had awoken to discover that the characters and situations of the dream-world I had inhabited existed in real life. I now understood the full seriousness of the action I had committed. For an instant I was very much afraid. I was trapped in a ghastly uncertainty. The trees of the glade seemed to close in on me. In my confusion I could see long worms sliding across the grass, leaving a slimy trail behind them. At that moment I feared I was going mad. I forced myself to concen-

trate on Sunil's worried face. Then, as I gazed at him, I became
aware that I loved him with a passion far deeper than I had
ever known could exist.

'Sunil, I will certainly join you,' I said. 'I will join you in
whatever place you go to. But I must prepare for the journey.
I must take just a few of my possessions I have always loved
—no more than will go into a saddle-bag. Please, Sunil, try to
understand.'

'Do you promise?' Sunil asked. 'Before the gods do you
promise you will join me? And love me? And live with me?'

'Yes, Sunil,' I answered. 'I promise.'

'Then you must listen carefully to me,' Sunil told me. 'For
a plan has come into my head. You know that Doshan is my
friend, but I do not wish to tell him the truth because he is a
servant of the Colonel Sahib, and it is dangerous. So please
listen to my plan. When I have reached my home in Ceylon,
my mother will be too much happy to see me, and she will
welcome me. And when I tell her about you she will wish to
welcome you also. And I know that you will like each other.
So then I will make a place ready for you—perhaps next to
our home. And when the place is all ready and prepared, I will
send my cousin as a guide to the Colonel Sahib's house. My
cousin lives in the fishing village of Dhanuskode on the straits.
When he has arrived, he will climb over the compound wall
where it joins the stables and he will tie a strip of blue cloth
to the weather-cock that is above the stables. When you see the
blue strip of cloth, you will know that the guide is waiting for
you. That night, when the Colonel Sahib is sleeping, you must
dress and go down into the yard. The guide will be hiding outside the compound near the wood. A horse for you will be
saddled and ready for the journey.'

The anxiety had left Sunil's face. He was calmer, and his eyes
were now alight with a steadfast love.

'When I get home tonight, what shall I say?' I asked him.

'Say to them that a mile or two away from the compound
I told you I was ill,' Sunil answered. 'Say to them you give me
leave to go back to the house.'

I went up to Sunil and kissed him on the forehead. He held

me close to his body and pressed his cheek against mine. With his arms around me I no longer felt afraid of the future.

'How long will it be?' I asked. 'Before your cousin will come for me?'

'Not long,' Sunil replied. 'Perhaps three weeks, no more. But now you must get on your horse and ride home.'

I kissed him on the lips. Then I turned away towards my horse. In silence, Sunil helped me to get into the saddle. He took my right hand and kissed the palm of it.

'Let your right hand remember my kiss until we meet again,' he said.

He stood gazing up at me. There were tears beneath the long lashes of his eyes.

'Now go, my darling,' he murmured. 'Yen anbé.'

'I love you,' I told him.

'May the gods help us both,' Sunil said. 'Anne, never forget. Look down at your right hand and know that in it lies Sunil's heart and soul. Now let me see you on your path back to the house.'

I tried to speak, but I could not. I turned my horse on to the homeward track. I looked round. Sunil had raised his hand and was staring after me. Then he leaped on to his horse and rode away.

———◆———

As I rode into the stableyard, Margaret appeared from the house.

'You're back late,' she said. 'Where's Sunil?'

'After we'd been riding for a while, Sunil told me he felt ill,' I replied. 'So I let him go home.'

Margaret listened intently.

'How long ago was that?' she asked.

'About two hours ago,' I answered. 'Isn't he back yet?'

'No, he's not back,' Margaret said. 'Where were you when Sunil told you that he was ill?'

I tried to think quickly. 'We'd got about half a mile along the track through the woods.'

'So Sunil turned round and rode straight back along the track?' Margaret asked.

'Yes,' I replied.

'But that's the way you must have returned,' Margaret said.

'Yes,' I answered. Even as I spoke I saw the trap into which I had fallen.

'Yet you didn't see Sunil?'

'No,' I answered.

'So he can't have had an accident,' Margaret said. 'And he hasn't come back to the house. And I can tell you exactly why. That boy wasn't ill at all. He was just making up an excuse. The boy was furious about the whipping he received. And I'll tell you what he's done. He's stolen the horse he was riding. He's run away with it.'

Margaret turned quickly and walked into the house.

16

I was sitting in my office adjoining the Mess. It was a bright pleasant room. I always enjoy looking at maps, so most of the wall-space is covered with maps of the district. Behind my desk hangs a large portrait of our Queen. I had just received an official letter from the Commander-in-Chief in which he congratulated me on the turn-out of my men, and I was feeling rather pleased with myself, when there was a knock at the door and, to my surprise, Kumar came in.

'What is it?' I asked.

'Memsahib, your sister, tell me to give you this,' Kumar said, handing me an envelope.

The letter was addressed to me in Margaret's handwriting. I tore it open and read its contents. The letter contained tiresome news. Young Sunil had made an excuse to leave Anne during their afternoon ride, saying he was ill and must go home. But he had not returned to the house. Margaret was convinced that Sunil had stolen the horse he rode—probably in revenge for the whipping he had been given. I thought rapidly. I was fairly certain that Sunil would not escape. We would catch up with him because my regiment had one of the best trackers in the district. But we must move fast.

'Tell the Memsahib I'll be back at the house in ten minutes,' I told Kumar. 'See that my saddle-bags are packed.'

Kumar salaamed and left. I got up from my desk, and opened the door that led into the Mess. Two officers were playing billiards. My Adjutant and a few other officers were sitting in leather armchairs, reading magazines. As I came in they all rose in greeting.

'Good evening,' I said to them. 'I think, gentlemen, I can offer you a little sport this evening. A hunt in fact.'

'Jackals?' Poole asked.

I smiled. 'No,' I replied. '*A* jackal. It seems that one of my syces has stolen a horse of mine, a chestnut gelding to be precise. The syce may have got two hours' start on us, so we'll just have to move quicker than he does. He may try to make for the straits. We'll take our tracker along with us. Well, gentlemen, any volunteers?'

Every officer raised his hand. I laughed.

'Thank you,' I said. I turned to Poole. 'I don't think we should be more than six in all,' I told him. 'We can't deplete the regiment of all its officers. So I'll leave that for you to organise. We'll rally outside my house in ten minutes' time.'

<hr/>

Margaret and Anne were in the drawing-room when I came back to the house. Anne was looking out of the window at the small cavalcade which was now assembling. When she swung round from the window I was dismayed by the expression on her face. Her eyes seemed strangely fixed, and she had somehow sucked in her lips so that her mouth was set in a thin line.

'Tom, what does it mean?' she asked.

'It means that little Sunil has stolen a horse,' I told her. 'We're going to hunt him down.'

Anne's face was now quite expressionless. 'And if you find him?' she asked.

'We'll put him under arrest,' I answered. 'And we'll hand him over to the police.'

Anne was silent. I turned to Margaret.

'Has Kumar packed my saddle-bags?' I asked.

'Yes,' Margaret answered. 'And I put in plenty of sandwiches in case you're away a long time.'

'Thank you,' I replied. 'Don't wait up for me. Good-night to you both.'

<hr/>

The tracker led us through the wood to the south of the house until he came to a glade where he dismounted and began to search around for hoof marks. He was a wizened little Indian of about sixty with deep-set eyes and a receding chin. His ability as a tracker was uncanny. I sometimes wondered if he did not rely as much on the weird instinct he possessed as on the evidence of his eyes. After he had examined the terrain for a while he came up to me quietly and gave me his report. I went to rejoin my officers.

'The tracker says three horses have been here,' I told them. 'But only one horse has been ridden in the direction of the straits, and it has been ridden fast. But the tracker knows a path which is a short-cut to Dhanuskode, the fishing-harbour where the boy has most probably gone to get some boat of sorts. It's a risk. But if we take the path there's a chance we'll get there before the jackal does.'

'Then let's take the path,' Poole said.

17

Anne had gone to bed and I was sitting alone in the drawing-room. I was holding up my petit-point to the light of the lamp and examining it, when there was a knock at the door and Kumar came in.

'Excuse, Memsahib,' he said. 'But Ashur Sahib, the secretary of His Highness the Rajah, is outside and asks if he may see you.'

'Isn't it rather late for a formal visit?' I asked.

'Ashur Sahib say it is urgent,' Kumar replied.

'Very well, Kumar,' I said. 'Show him in.'

I put aside my petit-point, and straightened my dress. I was standing by the mantelpiece when Kumar showed in Ashur and left. Ashur salaamed to me respectfully.

'Please forgive me for coming at this late hour,' Ashur said with a little simper of apology. 'But I come here at the command of His Highness.'

I inclined my head politely. I dislike Ashur. There is something sly and furtive about his thin pock-marked face.

'May I enquire where the Colonel Sahib is?' Ashur asked suddenly.

'As you probably know by now, one of the Colonel's syces has stolen a horse,' I told him. 'The Colonel and some of his officers are tracking down the syce.'

'Has the Colonel's Memsahib gone with them?' Ashur asked.

'No,' I replied. 'Mrs Carey has retired upstairs to her room.'

'It is better so,' Ashur said.

As Ashur glanced at me I saw a slight smirk of pleasure in his expression, and I was frightened.

'Why do you say that?' I asked.

'Do I have your leave to explain fully what has happened?' Ashur demanded.

'Certainly,' I replied. 'But I suggest you should sit down.'

Ashur sat himself in an armchair facing me. He cleared his throat. 'His Highness heard that the Colonel Sahib had ordered the young syce Sunil to be whipped,' Ashur began. Then he stopped as if he expected me to contradict him. 'This was an unusual thing to happen,' he continued. 'So His Highness wondered if the whipping had occurred because of some misdeed that Sunil had committed. For instance, perhaps Sunil had been bribed?'

Ashur paused. His small eyes were watching me closely. I gazed at him serenely.

'Bribed?' I asked. 'Who could have bribed him?'

'There is an English planter,' Ashur began. 'He has a bungalow beside the lake.'

'Rodney Meadows,' I said. 'What has he got to do with it? Anne has never even met him.'

Once again a little smirk flashed over Ashur's face.

'If you will forgive me for making such a remark,' Ashur said. 'That is not quite correct. The Memsahib has visited the bungalow more than once.'

He spoke with conviction. I could feel a dread spreading over me.

'She may have done,' I replied casually. 'I expect she forgot to tell me. But I still don't see what Rodney Meadows has got to do with the reason for your visit?'

'I was trying to explain,' Ashur said in a reproachful tone of voice. 'You ask me why Sunil should have been bribed. The reason might have been because someone wanted him not to tell about the Memsahib's visits to the bungalow.'

'Is that what His Highness thinks?' I enquired coldly.

'Yes,' Ashur replied. 'This was what he thought at one time. But he thinks this no longer.'

I rose from the chair. Anger was now overcoming my fear.

'Has His Highness sent you here to discuss the private affairs of the Colonel Sahib's wife?' I asked.

'I have been sent here to report an event which took place this very afternoon,' Ashur answered.

'What event?' I asked.

'I'm afraid that what I am forced to say will vex you very much,' Ashur told me.

'Let's hear what it is,' I replied. 'And then we'll see.' I was determined now to remain calm.

'I went riding this afternoon,' Ashur began, speaking quietly and deliberately.

'I never knew you were a horseman,' I remarked.

A trace of annoyance showed in Ashur's thin face.

'When my duties are done I go out riding,' he told me.

'I'm glad to hear it,' I said.

'This afternoon I was riding in the wood to the south of this house,' Ashur continued, speaking in an even and monotonous voice. 'My horse was walking slowly. But I did not care, for I was deep in my thoughts. Then, in the distance, I heard voices. The voices were talking quietly, and since there was nothing unusual about this, I moved forward.'

Ashur paused. I knew some of the devious ways of the Indian mind. I was convinced that Ashur had, for some reason, been sent out by the Rajah to spy on Anne.

'Did you dismount?' I asked briskly.

When Ashur hesitated I knew he was about to tell a lie.

'No,' Ashur replied. 'I stayed in the saddle. I let my horse walk along the little track it had been following. Then I reined in sharply.'

'Why?'

'Because ahead of me was a small glade in the wood. And lying in this little clearing were a girl and a young man. They were naked, and it was plain they had been making love. The two of them were lying naked together. The girl was European, and the young man was Indian. I first recognised the young man. It was the boy Sunil, your syce.'

Ashur paused again. He now sat motionless. He had the intentness of an animal of prey about to spring.

'The girl was the Colonel's Memsahib,' he said slowly. 'The Colonel Sahib's wife.'

I shook my head.

'I am afraid I don't believe you,' I told him. 'This story is some trick invented by the Rajah.'

'It is the truth,' Ashur answered quietly. 'And you know it is the truth. They were lying together naked in embrace. I sat there in the saddle without moving. I decided that I must turn round quietly in the direction from which I had come. But the boy Sunil must have sensed that he and the girl were not alone. Or perhaps he may have heard a noise as my horse shifted position. He leaped to his feet. He ran quickly towards me. He saw me. He recognised me. When he knew who I was, he must have been certain that I would tell the Rajah. He must have been very much afraid. I have proof of this. For this is the reason that Sunil has stolen the horse—the chestnut gelding. Sunil will move south. He will try to reach Dhanuskode on the straits. From there he can escape to Ceylon where his family live. He will cross over in a pathamari—the boats you call Dhows.'

Watching Ashur's face I was now certain that in the main he was telling the truth. Each phrase he had used added to the dismay and horror I now felt. I was aware that my mouth had begun to twitch. I raised my hand to cover it. When I spoke my voice sounded undisturbed.

'Why has His Highness sent you to tell me this?' I asked.

'Because His Highness thought that the Colonel Sahib should know the truth as soon as possible,' Ashur replied. 'He told me that he thought the Colonel Sahib should know that the girl he has brought from England to live in his house has been making love with a low caste syce.'

I was so angry that I could feel the blood swirling round in my head. But I knew that I must not for a single moment lose control of myself.

'Does anyone else know?' I asked.

'Only His Highness and myself.'

'Then will you give His Highness a message from me?' I asked Ashur. 'I know that animals only mate with their own species. But my message might be considered to be figurative. Will you please tell the Rajah that if in the jungle a strong tiger desired a young hind who had already found a partner to mate with, then, if this strong tiger discovered that the young hind had been taken by a jackal, the tiger should keep it a close secret. For otherwise all the beasts in his kingdom would laugh at him.'

Ashur inclined his head. 'The message is a wise one,' he said.

'Then please will you give the message to the Rajah?'

'Most certainly,' Ashur replied.

He rose to go, but I had not yet finished what I needed to say.

'You are the only person who witnessed what took place in the glade, are you not?' I asked.

'Indeed, yes,' Ashur answered.

'Are you acquainted with the law of slander?' I demanded. 'If not, I advise you to make enquiries into it. You will then discover that it is a very serious matter to impute the sin of adultery to a married woman. I think such an imputation might land you in considerable trouble.'

Ashur stared at me amazed. 'Do I understand that the Memsahib does not believe me?' he asked.

'Have you any proof?'

'No proof except my own eyes,' Ashur replied.

'But you are only one person,' I pointed out. 'I doubt if your evidence would be successful in a Court of Law—particularly if it were shown that you were in the pay of a man who was jealous of the Colonel Sahib's wife. And if you were found guilty, you might be sent to prison.'

'I still cannot understand what the Memsahib is trying to say,' Ashur announced.

'I'm giving you a warning,' I told him. 'At the moment, outside of this room, you and the Rajah are the only two people who are aware of the allegation you have made against the Colonel Sahib's wife. At this stage I very much doubt that my brother would contemplate bringing an action for slander. But were he to hear that the slander had been repeated by another person, then I am sure he would feel obliged to bring an action against you. Do you understand?'

'Yes,' Ashur replied. 'I do understand most clearly. And you and the Colonel may rest assured that such a situation will not arise. But in return, may I have your assurance that you will inform the Colonel Sahib of all I have told you?'

'Yes,' I replied.

He moved to the door and opened it.

'May I have your permission to take my leave?' Ashur asked.

'Certainly,' I answered. 'Good-night.'

Ashur salaamed. 'Good-night, Memsahib,' he said, and left the room.

After he had gone, I sat at the solitaire board which was placed on a little table by the fireside. Slowly I began to play, trying to collect my thoughts.

The Rajah was jealous of Anne, and he had set Ashur to spy on her. That much was certain. Ashur had discovered Anne and Sunil in a glade in the wood. He had found them in the act of love. However much the idea revolted and shocked me I must now admit the truth. Sunil had discovered that Ashur had been spying on the two of them. Sunil had decided to escape from inevitable retribution. He had ridden off south on the chestnut gelding. He must have had almost two hours' start, so it was unlikely that Tom would catch him. Obviously Sunil had been forced to leave Anne behind. For however low Anne might have sunk she must still have had the sense to realise that she could not elope with a cheap little Indian groom. And Anne was now lying upstairs in Tom's bedroom. She must know that Ashur would tell the Rajah. Her only hope could be that the Rajah would never tell Tom.

My fingers now seemed to be moving automatically. I soon finished the game. I rose and put a log on the fire, then I added another, for I knew that a long evening lay ahead of me.

Though I was filled with disgust and anger when I thought of what Anne had done, I could not help feeling sorry for her. She had put herself in a terrible position. In time, Tom might or might not forgive her. But he would never forget. Moreover, Tom was highly sensitive to the opinion of his officers. He enjoyed their admiration. And for the next few months he would most surely be haunted by the possibility that someone in the palace might gossip about Anne and that the shameful truth would become common knowledge. For a while I thought of going up to Anne's bedroom in order to warn her. But what good would that do? Anne would then have to wait in suspense, hour after hour, for Tom's return and for the scene between them which now seemed unavoidable. Though I had not been fond of Anne at first, I had come to like her. In addition, I was aware of the misery it would cause Tom if, in his anger, he were to send Anne away. I knew that Tom and I could never live happily alone together again. Those days were past for ever.

When Anne first came out to Telacamund, I tried, perhaps unconsciously, to show her in a bad light, because in the back of my mind was fixed the desire to get rid of her. I now could appreciate that my only hope of living in peace with Tom was to keep Anne in the house. Should I therefore say nothing to Tom about Ashur's visit? But the risk was too great. I *must* tell Tom the truth, because, if I concealed it, the Rajah in his subtle manner might find out that I had not repeated Ashur's message and might confront Tom with the facts. Further, there was now, I realised, the grim chance that Anne might have a child by Sunil. Once more, the girl's total disregard for the consequences of her behaviour began to enrage me. But I must overcome my anger.

I put the coloured marbles in place on the solitaire board, and once more I began to play. Presently a plan came into my mind which might solve my difficulty. And I began to ponder over the situation yet again.

18

Clouds were covering the moon, but the track along which we moved was plainly visible. As we rode through the valley which led to the village of Dhanuskode, we saw my chestnut gelding hobbling towards us. Sunil must have lamed him on some stretch of rough ground. Young Phillips stayed behind to examine the poor brute. The rest of us galloped on towards the village. We reached a rickety wooden landing stage, but there was no boat there. While we stood by the shore, the moon came out from behind the clouds and shone clearly on to the straits. The sea was very smooth. In the far distance we could see a small pathamari sailing towards Ceylon.

'If Sunil's on that boat, then it's the last we shall see of him,' I said.

'Can't we find a fishing boat of some kind and give chase?' Rigg asked.

'It's too late,' I told him. 'By the time we had got the boat, I'm afraid that the pathamari will have reached harbour.'

Our tracker had been talking to a villager, a grey-haired fisherman. He now came up to me and spoke in English so that the fisherman would not understand him.

'This man tells me he has seen no stranger in the village or on the shore all evening,' the tracker said. Then he pointed to the little boat on the moonlit waters. 'But I think he lies,' the tracker continued. 'I think Sunil is on that boat.'

'Then there's no more we can do,' I announced.

Poole and Frank Russell, who had ridden into the village, now rejoined us.

'We've searched inside every single house and hovel,' Poole said. 'But he's nowhere there.'

I pointed to the pathamari. 'Sunil has escaped on that boat,' I told them. 'We can't catch up with it now. We'd better head back for home. Sorry, gentlemen. But I'm afraid our jackal has escaped us.'

———◆◆◆———

Margaret was standing by the fireside when I came in. I crossed the room and embraced her.

'You shouldn't have waited up for me,' I told her.

'I can't sleep,' Margaret replied. 'Did you catch Sunil?'

'No,' I answered. 'But I saw a pathamari more than half way across the straits. He must have got on board over an hour before we arrived. We found the horse, lamed, quite close to the harbour.'

'Have you any suspicion why Sunil stole your horse and escaped?' Margaret asked.

'Because he's a dishonest rogue,' I told her.

'You can't think of any other reason?' Margaret enquired.

I took a sip of the drink that Kumar had brought me from the dining-room. 'None at present,' I replied.

Margaret sat down in her armchair by the fire. Her mouth had begun twitching and she covered it with her hand.

'You're tired,' I told her. 'You should go to bed.'

'I'll wait until you have finished your drink,' Margaret answered.

For a moment there was silence.

'The Rajah's secretary, Ashur, called at the house late this evening,' Margaret announced slowly.

'What did he want?' I asked.

'Ashur had been ordered by the Rajah to spy on Anne,' Margaret said.

'Why?'

'I suppose the Rajah is jealous of her. He had an idea that each time Anne went out riding it was to keep a secret assignation.'

'And was it?' I asked. 'Was it an assignation?'

'No,' Margaret answered. 'It wasn't.'

'So why did Ashur come here?'

Margaret hesitated. 'He came here with an extremely unpleasant tale,' she said.

'What tale?'

'His outrageous story is that when Anne went out riding with Sunil this afternoon, he followed them. Ashur followed them until they came to a clearing in the wood. He says that Sunil tethered the horses. Now comes the disgusting part of his story. Ashur maintains that Anne and Sunil took off their clothes and made love.'

The flagrant impudence which the Rajah had displayed in sending Ashur to my house to tell such a lie to Margaret made me furious.

'And who tells you this?' I cried out. 'Ashur, a dishonest crook, one of the Rajah's spies. Don't you understand? The Rajah wants me to get rid of Anne so he can have a chance of getting her for himself. The Rajah hears that Sunil has run off with one of my horses. So he invents a cunning lie to fit in with the event.'

'That would appear to be the case,' Margaret replied quietly.

'Well, I don't believe a word of it,' I said. 'And I'm ashamed now that I ever allowed myself to suspect that Anne could be capable of demeaning herself with Sunil. Anne would never make love to a common little syce. As you know, when the stables were dirty, I was in her sitting-room while I had Sunil whipped. And I was watching her to see if she had developed some stupid girlish passion for the boy. But when I had seen her face I was convinced I was wrong.'

'And I presume that you're still convinced?'

'Certainly,' I replied.

'I must admit that Ashur told his story with great assurance,' Margaret said.

'But you don't believe it, do you?' I asked.

'Ashur appeared to be so sure of himself that I had to warn him that if he ever repeated his story again, you would sue him for slander,' Margaret replied.

Suddenly I was suspicious.

'You haven't answered my question,' I pointed out.

'I'm tired and my brain is quite confused,' Margaret announced. 'There doesn't seem to me to be any question about it. All that's important is to make sure that Ashur is silenced effectively by my threat of an action for slander.'

'So you don't believe Ashur's story?' I persisted.

As Margaret raised her head I saw that her face was quivering with fatigue.

'Ashur's a spy,' Margaret said. 'And he's probably a born liar.'

'Do you think he was impressed by your threat of an action?' I asked.

'Yes,' Margaret answered. 'Yes, most certainly.'

I could see from Margaret's face that she was completely exhausted. But never before in my life had I found her so confused. I glanced at her covertly. With a sense of shock I realised that she had aged terribly. My sister now pointed her thin, delicately lined face towards me. Her worn eyes seemed full of an unusual look of entreaty.

'But there's just one thing I must ask you" she told me.

'What's that?'

'I don't want Anne to know about Ashur's visit,' Margaret said.

'Why not?' I asked. 'Surely it's safer to warn her of the Rajah's lies and deceit?'

'I don't agree with you,' Margaret replied. 'I think that if Anne knew that Ashur had been here, and if she knew the story he had told us, she would be most desperately upset. What's more, she would be afraid that the gossip might spread. So I'm convinced it's better that we don't tell her a word about Ashur's unpleasant visit. Please take my advice, Tom. When you go upstairs, if Anne's awake, then just tell her simply that you followed Sunil to the fishing-village and found that Sunil had sailed across the straits in a boat, and leave it at that.'

I finished my drink. I reflected that Margaret might well be correct in her assessment of Anne's reaction to Ashur's filthy lie.

'Will you take my advice?' Margaret asked.

'Yes,' I answered.

I put down my glass and crossed the room and kissed Margaret's forehead.

'And now,' I said, 'I think we should both go upstairs to our beds.'

Anne was still awake when I came into the bedroom.

'Did you find him?' she asked.

Her voice was expressionless, but her eyes were searching my face anxiously. Obviously, she had grown quite fond of Sunil. But I would not blame her.

'Sunil has escaped,' I told her. 'We tracked him as far as a fishing-village on the straits. But he'd managed to get on a little boat that was sailing across to Ceylon. So I don't suppose we will ever see him again. You'll have to go out riding with Doshan in future.'

Anne did not speak. By the light of the lamp her eyes seemed very large as they stared at me.

'Incidentally, we found the chestnut gelding,' I said. 'It had been lamed. I'll arrange to send for the vet in the morning.'

'How do you know that Sunil had got on to a fishing-boat?' Anne asked.

'We don't know for certain,' I answered. 'But he definitely wasn't in the village. So we presumed he'd crossed over to Ceylon where his family comes from.'

I bent down and kissed Anne's cheek. 'You look almost worn out, and I'm completely exhausted,' I told her. 'So I'll sleep in the dressing-room.'

19

At first I felt guilty that in a way I had attempted to deceive Tom by letting him suppose that I believed Ashur's story to be untrue. I consoled myself with the thought that if Tom had known I was convinced that Anne had slept with Sunil he would have confronted Anne, and she might have broken down and confessed. No one knows Tom as well as I do. I am certain that if he had found out the truth he would have been not only furious but utterly disgusted, and his attitude towards Anne would never be the same again.

I now had only one fear—the possibility that Anne might have a child and that Sunil might be the child's father. This fear of mine increased as the days passed by, for Anne had recently told us that she was feeling ill and would not go out riding for a while. Indeed Anne does look unwell. She moves restlessly about the house and seldom visits her sitting-room.

One evening after dinner when we were alone together I decided that I must once again talk to Anne seriously. It was a good moment to choose because Anne appeared to be far more cheerful than she had been for some time.

'I don't want to pry into the secrets you share with Tom,' I began. 'And I don't want you to think I'm trying to thrust myself into your confidence. But though I'm a spinster I do have a certain knowledge of the world. And my instinct tells me that I might well be able to help you. For instance, you've been looking pale and ill this last fortnight. And I wonder if the reason might be a very simple one?'

'I did think . . .' Anne began, and then stopped.

'What did you think?' I asked her softly.

'I thought I was going to have a child,' Anne blurted out. 'But it's now certain I'm not pregnant.'

'You're really sure about that, are you?' I asked.

'Yes,' Anne replied. 'Completely sure.'

'I'd like to ask you a great favour,' I said. 'If you find that you are pregnant, will you please confide in me?' I tried to smile. 'As I expect you know, I had hospital training before I came out here. So I might even be able to give you some advice.'

'Very well,' Anne replied. 'I *will* tell you. And thank you for your kindness. I'm afraid I must have got on your nerves by being so moody these last few days. You've been wonderfully patient with me. But I'm feeling better now. Tomorrow I might even go for a ride in the afternoon.'

'I'm delighted to hear it,' I answered. 'But speaking of riding—I don't want to seem impertinent, but I think I should tell you that even though it's perfectly innocent I don't think you should visit Rodney Meadows. He's not well thought of by the English community.'

Anne was staring at me.

'How do you know I visited Rodney Meadows?' she asked me.

I gave her a smile of reassurance. 'I hear all kinds of things,' I said lightly. 'But I don't repeat them. Not even to Tom. And that's the reason why I don't want you to visit Rodney Meadows—because I think Tom would be displeased if he ever heard about it.'

'Thank you for the warning,' Anne murmured.

Tom found a young syce called Mohan who was a few years older than Sunil and a hard worker. But Anne obstinately refused to go out riding with Doshan or the new lad. She would now spend hours on end in her sitting-room. Once when I came into the room unexpectedly she was staring out of the window. There was not even a sheet of paper on her desk. I was worried about Anne. Surely she must know that Sunil had left her for good and there was nothing she could do.

One day at lunch she put down her knife and fork and gazed up at Tom with a look of wild entreaty.

'Tom,' she asked quietly, 'if I promise not to take the track up into the hills, if I promise to stay on the path and never leave the lake-side, then please can I go out riding alone?'

Tom hesitated. Then he looked up at her wan quivering face.

'Yes,' he replied. 'But would it really worry you if Doshan rode about ten lengths behind you?'

'That's it,' Anne answered. 'That's just it. Some parts of the day I like to be alone. And I don't feel alone if there's a groom riding behind me. I can't explain why. But there it is. If I can't go out riding alone, I shan't go out riding at all.'

'Very well,' Tom said. 'You can go out alone this very afternoon.'

———◆◆◆———

Anne returned earlier than usual that evening. She looked less distraught. But as we sat in the drawing-room later that night I watched her as she read a novel by Thackeray that she had taken from the library. Presently I noticed that she had not turned over a page for some ten minutes. I looked at her eyes. They were glazed in abstraction. She looked desperately tired. I was not surprised when she rose and announced that she was going to bed. Tom entered the drawing-room soon afterwards. I decided that I could conceal my worries about Anne no longer.

'I'm afraid that Anne is unwell,' I told him. 'She's not ill in her body, she's ill in her mind.'

I had expected Tom to disagree with me violently. But he stared down at the carpet in silence.

'Do you know what's wrong?' I asked quietly.

'No, I don't,' he replied. 'I only wish I did. She's grown strange. When she's alone with me, she's oddly submissive— far more than she used to be. But at the same time she's aloof. In a way I find hard to describe, she manages to make me feel almost guilty whenever I make love to her. As a result, most nights I sleep in my dressing-room.'

I was silent. Obviously I could think of a reason why Anne no longer wished to sleep with her husband. But Sunil had left her a month ago. Surely Anne could not still be pining for him? As I looked at Tom's stricken face I was tempted to tell him the truth. But what good would it do? Sunil had left. In time Anne would get over her passion for him. Gradually her relationship with Tom would improve. It was not Anne's emotions that I was worried about, but her state of mind.

'Let's hope it's just a passing phase,' I said to Tom. 'I believe that in a week or so she will settle down again.'

20

I try hard to avoid going into my sitting-room, but I'm constantly drawn to it. And I know the reason why. From the window I can see the weather-cock. I cannot stop myself looking at it. I close my eyes and pray that when I open them again I will see a blue strip of cloth fluttering in the breeze.

If Tom's information was correct, Sunil sailed to Ceylon from the fishing-village of Dhanuskodi over four weeks ago. Sunil promised me that the guide would arrive in three weeks' time. What has gone wrong? Is it possible that Tom lied to me? Could Tom and his friends have caught Sunil and handed him over to the police? Could Sunil be imprisoned in some jail? Yet why should Tom lie to me? After all, he does not suspect that I'm in love with Sunil. And if Sunil were in jail, would he not find some method of sending a message to me?

Each day the suspense of waiting grows worse. Sometimes when I look at the weather-cock, for an instant I believe I can see a strip of blue cloth tied to it. Then I realise it is only a trick of the light.

———◄◆►———

This morning as I sat at my desk, gazing out at the yard, Doshan passed by. When he saw me he stopped. He looked round to make sure no one was watching, then he inclined his head slightly and moved off towards the stables. It was a clear invitation for me to join him. Luckily Margaret was out. I could feel my heart beating as I walked through the hall. I thought it must mean there was some news of Sunil.

I found Doshan grooming Cara. He put down the curry-comb and slid his hand into his pocket and produced an envelope. He handed it to me.

'For the Memsahib,' he said.

'Thank you, Doshan,' I replied.

I looked at the envelope. There was no writing on it. I folded it carefully and tucked it into my blouse.

'Thank you, Doshan,' I repeated.

I hurried back to the house. In my sitting-room I opened the letter.

'Dear Anne,' it began, 'please could you come and see me as soon as possible.'

The letter was signed: 'Rodney.'

When I arrived outside Rodney's bungalow, a bearer was waiting by the gate in the compound. He helped me to dismount, tethered my horse, and led me up to the verandah. At that moment Rodney appeared.

'Good afternoon,' Rodney said to me. 'Do you mind if we don't sit on the verandah because any passer-by may see us, and I'm rather anxious you shouldn't be seen with me. So if you're agreeable, I'll offer you a glass of wine in my living-room.'

The outside of the house was decrepit; I was pleasantly surprised when I found that, inside, it was clean and attractively furnished. Bowls of roses stood on plain oak tables. A log was burning in the open fire-place. The long room was unpretentious yet distinguished.

'I received your letter,' I told Rodney. 'I've taken a slight risk in coming here because my previous visits were reported to Margaret.'

'Who in heaven's name could have told her?' Rodney asked as he poured out two glasses of wine.

'I can't imagine,' I replied.

There was a pause. Rodney was watching me as he sipped his drink.

'I expect you wonder why I sent you that note?' Rodney said. 'What did you think when you received it?'

He was smiling at me. His attitude was rather strange, and as he walked up and down the room I noticed that his movements were clumsy. When I looked at his eyes, I saw that they were bloodshot. He was not yet drunk, but he had been drinking heavily.

'What did you think?' Rodney repeated.

'I thought you might have a message for me,' I answered quietly.

I took a sip of wine. Suddenly Rodney laughed. As he laughed, his hand jerked and he spilt his drink on the carpet. Immediately he went to the sideboard and refilled his glass.

'Now why ever should I have a message for you?' he asked.

As he spoke, my hope of hearing at last from Sunil vanished.

'When you said you wished to see me as soon as possible I presumed that you might have a message for me,' I repeated.

'A message! A message from whom? What romantic ideas you do have!' Rodney exclaimed still smiling.

'Then may I ask why you *did* invite me to come here?' I enquired.

'Because it's essential that I should talk to you,' Rodney answered.

At that moment a wild idea came into my head. Supposing that Rodney were teasing me? Supposing Sunil had escaped from prison or had not returned to Ceylon, then he might be hiding in Rodney's bungalow. After all, Rodney was in love with an Indian girl. He might therefore be capable of understanding the love that existed between Sunil and myself. And what else would Rodney have to talk to me about? I could feel a tension in my breast when I thought that at any moment I might see my darling Sunil again. Or perhaps Rodney had somehow found out news of him. I so much wanted to hear the truth that I could hardly restrain my impatience. Even if Rodney had only got some vague report about Sunil's movements I would be glad. For it would give me the opportunity to reveal to someone who would probably be understanding the intense love that was consuming me. But then I glanced at the tall man who was shambling awkwardly around the room, and a cold fear of doubt invaded me. Quite apart from the fact that he had been drinking hard, there now seemed something definitely odd about him. His presence somehow jarred on my nerves. I no longer trusted him. There was a sly expression on his face together with a look of complicity as if we both shared some unpleasant secret. Before, Rodney had been dignified and aloof in my presence, whereas now he was familiar, almost disrespectful.

'What is it you wish to talk to me about?' I asked.

'Yourself,' he said. 'And myself, in various ways and various aspects.'

'I'm afraid I don't understand,' I muttered.

'I daresay you don't,' Rodney answered. 'I'm not surprised. I didn't think you *would* understand—or at least not at first. So let's start with your problems. Now what about young Sunil? He's an attractive boy is young Sunil—as I'm sure you will agree. I'm told that the girls down in Telacamund village are quite enamoured of him.'

I now began to feel that Rodney was playing a game with me.

'At the time,' Rodney continued, 'I must confess that I rather wondered why all of a sudden you stopped visiting me. You never even rode past the compound.'

'The answer to that is quite simple, and I've already told it to you,' I replied. 'Margaret had heard that I'd been coming here and warned me against doing so because it seems that you're not very well thought of by the British community.'

'I wonder if that was the only reason why your visits ceased,' Rodney said. 'I have a curious feeling that it had more to do with the behaviour of young Sunil.'

'I still don't understand what you're talking about,' I replied.

'Well, as I told you, a tea-planter has plenty of leisure,' Rodney said. 'So recently I've spent a little time putting various facts together. I assembled them in my mind like a human jigsaw. The first fact which I found rather odd was that I heard Sunil had been whipped. Now I had observed Sunil fairly closely—as I do all unusually beautiful specimens of humanity. And I decided that not only was he an extremely charming boy, but he was obviously a competent syce. So why should he have been whipped? What fault had he committed?'

Rodney was staring at me with his bloodshot eyes. His glass was empty, and he refilled it.

'Perhaps you can provide an answer to that question?' he enquired.

'Yes, I can,' I replied. 'Tom made an inspection of the stables and decided that Sunil had been slacking in his work, so he had Sunil whipped.'

'And had Sunil been slacking?'

'I can't tell you,' I answered. 'I don't visit the stables.'

'The next fact that interested me was Sunil's departure,' Rodney continued. 'Sunil, it seems, stole one of your husband's horses, escaped to the village of Dhunaskode and sailed away to Ceylon. Now I wonder what inspired him to do such a thing? That's another question you can answer for me.'

'I'm sorry, but I can't,' I replied. 'I only know that Sunil stole a horse and that my husband gave chase and failed to catch him.'

Rodney peered at me over his glass.

'You've been ill recently, haven't you?' he asked gently. 'You still don't look well. I'm afraid, my dear Anne, that you are very unhappy. And I think I know the reason why. Last week I paid a visit to the village of Dhunaskode. Sunil has a cousin in that village. Did you know?'

'No,' I replied.

'It was Sunil's cousin who helped him to find a boat to escape in,' Rodney said. 'You see, he's a fisherman. And he appears to be fond of Sunil. Yet when I questioned him about the boy, the fisherman became strangely reticent. I could hardly get one word out of him. However, as soon as I had returned to my bungalow I began putting my jigsaw together. And now I've constructed a picture of sorts. But I wonder if it's a true picture? Is it?'

'Did you invite me here merely to ask me that question?' I enquired.

'No,' Rodney answered. 'I wanted you to come here because I think you may need help.'

Rodney leaned against the back of an armchair and stood gazing at me.

'I'm being clumsy,' he mumbled. 'Even before you arrived this afternoon I was afraid I would be clumsy. Please forgive me. I know that what I'm now going to say will hurt your feelings. I wish I could think of some other way of putting it. But I'm afraid I must say it straight out and risk your anger. I'm very fond of you, Anne. I admire you very much. I respect your feelings. I must inform you that I know the truth. So I'm aware that there's an event which might possibly occur.'

Rodney stopped. Into the bleary expression of his eyes there came an unexpected look of tenderness.

'If that event did occur,' he said in a quiet voice, 'then it might mean that you'd need my help. Remember you've been ill these last few weeks. So what if you have a child? And what if the child is born with a coloured skin?'

I rose from my chair. I could feel the blood rushing to my face. I was now certain that Rodney knew all about Sunil and me.

'You've drunk too much wine,' I said to Rodney. 'I think I should go.'

Rodney did not move. He was still staring at me.

'You won't go,' he said. 'You won't go because you're perfectly aware that I know the truth. If your child was born with a coloured skin, then I don't think you could go on living with your husband at Mickleden. And you could hardly go back to your parents in England with a coloured baby in your arms. So I could help you. I could help you by inviting you and your child to come and live here with me in this house.'

I looked at him in astonishment. I still could not appreciate the import of what he had said. I was silent.

'I would be very glad to be responsible for looking after your child,' Rodney stated.

I gaped at him in bewilderment. I could think of nothing to say. I was already certain that Sunil had not given me a child. But it now seemed futile to persist in denying my relationship with him. Rodney seemed anxious to be friendly. And I needed a friend.

'You see, my life has changed somewhat since we last met,' Rodney continued. 'I must tell you that my little Theivaney has left me. A young Indian came up on holiday from Madras and fell in love with the girl. The boy's parents own a large paper-factory in the state of Madras. So Theivaney's parents decided that the young man would be a more suitable match for their daughter than myself. And Theivaney fancied him. So now she's gone. She's left me for good. The house now seems rather large and very empty.'

Rodney filled up our glasses. I noticed that his hands were no longer shaking. I thought it was very kind of Rodney to offer his house as a refuge. But there were many reasons why I could not accept the offer. I decided, however, to tell him the truth about Sunil.

'It's true that I love Sunil,' I told Rodney. 'But I'm not pregnant. I'm very grateful for your offer. But Sunil could never come here.'

Rodney stared at me in amazement.

'Have you gone mad?' he asked. 'You looked quite distracted when you arrived here. Have you been listening to a word I've said? Or haven't I made myself clear? I'm not interested in your affair with Sunil. It's you that I'm interested in. Let me put it plainly. I'm very lonely here. I want you to come and live with me. I'm not suggesting we should be lovers. But I need your presence. Above all, I want you as a friend.'

I watched Rodney in consternation. For a moment I thought he must be completely drunk. But he was gazing at me steadily, and he obviously meant what he had said.

'How could I possibly come and live in this bungalow?' I asked. 'Even if I decided to leave my husband, I couldn't come here. I still have some respect for him. I don't want to hurt and humiliate him gratuitously.'

'Would that be the effect of your decision to live with me?'

'Yes,' I answered quietly. 'I'm afraid so. If I left my husband, I would leave this country altogether.'

'And go where?' Rodney enquired. As he spoke he finished his glass of wine and went to the sideboard to refill it. Suddenly he turned. 'You wouldn't be such an idiot as to consider joining the boy in Ceylon?' he asked.

Once again I was silent. I could not bring myself to lie to him. Slowly Rodney shook his head. 'You poor benighted fool!' he cried. 'No wonder that when I first saw you this afternoon I thought you looked mad. You must be totally insane if you even *consider* going to live with that boy in his village in Ceylon.'

'Why?'

'Do you realise what the life would be like? Have you no idea? I suppose they would build some kind of mud-hut for you and the boy to live in. But do you think you'd have any privacy? I know the life of an Indian village. So I can give you the answer. None. Sunil's mother and aunts and brothers and sisters will come swarming in to call on you, and you'll have to be polite to them while they chat in Tamil for hours on end. There'll be no running water. No sanitation. Goats and hens will wander into your room and defecate. Sacred cows will eat what few crops you have got. Flies will cluster around every morsel of food you raise to your lips. And what will you have at the end of it? Your true love, you may answer. But how long will he continue to be your true love? Make no mistake about this. The Sunil with whom you'll be living in a village in Ceylon will be a very different young man from the obedient and adoring boy who was your syce here in Telacamund. After the first few rapturous days, you'll find that he wants to go out with his friends. If they have any money, they will probably get drunk at the village stores. And if you protest when he returns late, he'll give you a beating—because that's the way that wives or concubines are treated.'

Rodney moved across and gently touched my hand.

'I'm sorry, Anne,' he murmured. 'I don't want to make you unhappy. But I must force you to face reality, because evidently you have no idea of the kind of life you'd have to lead out there.'

'If my love for Sunil were sufficiently strong,' I said, 'wouldn't I grow used to the life in the course of time?'

'No,' Rodney answered. 'I don't think you would.'

'I may still decide to try,' I replied.

Rodney smiled, and for a moment he looked young.

'You're a very obstinate person,' he told me. 'Yet I'm fond of you just the same. But you're looking desperately tired, so do please at least sit down.'

I did indeed feel weary so I sat down in the armchair opposite him.

'Do you remember the lecture you gave me about England's snobbery in India?' I asked him.

'I do indeed,' he replied.

'Well, holding the principles that you do,' I said, 'I would have thought that you would have encouraged me to live in a village in Ceylon. I'd have thought that you'd consider it a step in the right direction—a step towards removing the barrier which divides us from the Indians.'

Rodney was silent for a while. He was no longer looking at me. His hands were clasped together and he was gazing down at them.

'You know, I can remember very well what I said to you about the snobbery of England and the gulf between us and the Indians,' he began. ' "Barrier" was the word *you* used. Well, I've been thinking about this barrier, and I've come to an odd conclusion. Let me try to explain. I believe that all of us have faults in our nature which we can't control and which we never will be able to control. And it's these faults that form the real barrier between us and other human beings. The superficial barrier of colour merely obscures this fundamental reality.'

Rodney paused. He took out a silk handkerchief from his pocket and began playing with it absent-mindedly, running it between his fingers.

'There have always existed and there still exist obvious barriers between members of the human race—owner and slaves, master and servant, Captain and deck-hand,' he continued. 'There are any number of such divisions. But by the passing of a law or by a change of circumstances these divisions can considerably be overcome. It is within each one of us that there exists the *permanent* barrier. It's this innate barrier which will forever separate us from our neighbour—whatever rank or colour or caste the neighbour may be. The trouble is that essentially we are bigoted. Each one of us is devoted to his prejudices or predilections. These form part of the barrier that we have erected inside us. So really it's hypocrisy to pretend that we admire or that we despise the coloured races. What kind of man do we despise and from which coloured race, we should ask ourselves? More important, will our inner barrier extend to him or will it not? Let us meet the person concerned. Let us appraise him or her. But let our appraisal be honest. God made us all equal. And if we dislike some pock-marked Indian or some gross negro, before we pass judgment, let us make certain that we would not be just as censorious if the very same person but with a white skin came begging at our back door in Sussex. The truth is that the only important barrier exists in our own souls.'

Rodney tied a knot in his handkerchief and looked up at me and smiled.

'The knot is to remind me not to drink so much tomorrow,' he said. 'I'm really getting quite drunk. But you can have no idea how lonely I've been these last few weeks. Your presence in itself is enough to intoxicate me. So please try to bear with my confused thoughts. You see, quite apart from obvious reasons, I think I can understand why I'm so fond of you. There's a particular quality which joins some of us in the human race. But it's not—as we might like to think it—love or hate, or strength or weakness. Certainly it's not weakness. For the weak will never inherit the earth, nor will the humble and meek. Make no mistake about it. That concept was perhaps the most fraudulent prospectus ever presented to the public. What joins you and me and a few others of our kind together is the ability to feel and suffer. Call it sentimentality if you like. But it's this quality that unites us—red or brown or yellow or black or white. We're joined together by the fact that we have no hope of avoiding each other's misery. But we're an ineffectual bunch. Our word will never prevail. So the strong and blunt and ambitious will continue to rule the earth until the whole orbit shrivels and becomes just a speck in the universe.'

Rodney got up and poured himself a glass of wine. Then he sat down again.

'I'm so drunk now that I don't think I can possibly get any drunker,' he explained. Then he stumbled towards me. 'I'm not much to look at, and I'm pretty hopeless at times, I admit it,' he said. 'But I have this tremendously strong instinct which tells me that we'd get on together. Please, Anne, please come and live with me.'

'You know it's impossible,' I told him. 'But I'm sure there must be plenty of other people for you to choose from.'

'You mean I should find another Theivaney?'

'Perhaps,' I replied. 'If you thought she could bring you happiness.'

Suddenly Rodney's whole expression changed. He began to tremble. His long face seemed to swell as the angry words spurted out from him.

'So you want me to buy a girl from the bazaar?' he cried. 'That's the way you want to get out of it. That's your clever suggestion so you can avoid coming to live here. Why not say straight out that you can't bear the sight of me?'

'Because it's not true,' I replied. But he was no longer listening to me. His whole personality seemed to have changed.

'Why not tell me that I'm just a middle-aged drunk with no hope left in the world?' he shouted. 'Why not tell me that I revolt you? Why not proclaim that I'm a failure and that I've failed in every single relationship I've ever had in my life and in every single thing I've attempted to do?'

As I looked at him I saw tears coming into his eyes. His face was now twisted with misery. I felt great pity for him. Without thinking I moved across to him and put my hand on his cheek.

'I'm sorry I've offended you, Rodney,' I said. 'I didn't mean to—because I'm very fond of you.'

Violently he brushed my hand aside.

'I don't want your pity,' he cried out. 'Who asked you to pity me? Go back to your husband. Or go back to your little Indian boy. But for Christ's sake leave me alone.'

Then Rodney covered his face with his hands and began to sob.

'Please go,' he gasped out.

His shoulders were shaking as if he had a fever when I left the room.

21

'Did you enjoy your ride?' I asked Anne that evening before dinner.

'Yes,' Anne replied calmly. 'It was a beautiful afternoon.'

I glanced at her, later, as she ate the Madras curry which our cook always prepared so well and which Anne seems to be growing to like. Her expression was serene without the slightest trace of guilt. I should probably never know if Anne has visited Rodney Meadows because the source of information I had established after Ashur's evening call on me had dried up. My source had illustrated to me yet again the way in which news travels in India. Though apparently devious, it was quite simple. The librarian's Indian clerk knew the elder sister of the Indian girl who lived with Rodney Meadows, and he had sought to ingratiate himself with me for various reasons by volunteering to pass on information. But now the Indian girl had gone. Besides, I felt ashamed of myself for doubting Anne's promise. But her behaviour with Sunil had made me suspicious, and I was determined to avoid the possibility of a scandal.

'Will you go out riding tomorrow?' I asked.

Anne looked straight into my eyes. 'I may do,' she answered casually. 'Unless, of course, there's a polo match or some function you'd like me to attend.'

It is now over six weeks since Sunil escaped to Ceylon. I am virtually certain that Anne has received no communication from him. Surely she must realise that she will never see him again. Yet far from decreasing, her restlessness has grown worse. Whereas a month ago she scarcely visited her sitting-room, she now spends almost all day enclosed in that little den. Whenever I come in, I find her sitting at her desk, staring across the yard. I'd have thought that her gaze would have been fixed on the stables where little Sunil used to work, but her eyes seem to be concentrated on the sky immediately above the roof. And after dinner, when she is with me in the drawing-room, Anne seldom bothers even to pretend to be reading her library book. She has adopted a particular mannerism. She will stretch out her right hand on her lap, palm upwards, and remain for hours on end examining it intently, as if the outline of each finger and the shape of her wrist were a matter of deep importance. This mannerism disturbed me so much that I felt obliged to ask Anne about it.

'Does your hand hurt you?' I enquired gently.

'No,' Anne answered in surprise. 'Why should it?'

'Because you keep staring down at it,' I told her.

Anne blinked nervously. 'Do I?' she asked. 'I didn't realise it. I'm sorry.'

'There's no need to be sorry,' I told her. 'We all have our little mannerisms. I'm sure I'm the worst offender. But I must tell you the truth, my dear Anne. I'm worried about you.'

'Why?' Anne asked.

It occurred to me that the moment had now come for Anne to confide in me about Sunil if she so wished. I would not force her confidence. But I believed that if she confessed the truth to me, it might relieve the tension in her mind.

'I'm worried about you,' I told Anne, 'because I think that you're very unhappy.'

Anne was silent. She had covered her right hand with her left. She looked completely distraught.

'You never know,' I said lightly. 'I might be able to help you.'

'You're very kind,' Anne replied. 'And I am grateful to you. Really I am. Please, Margaret, please remember what I am saying to you now. I understand what you feel about me— perhaps better than you think. At first you disliked me. But during the last two months you've grown to be fond of me.

I'm aware of it. I can sense it with all my being. And I'm fond of you too, though you might not believe it. You've been kind to me. And I am deeply grateful to you and I always will be. Please remember what I am saying. Remember it—whatever happens.'

' "Whatever happens," ' I repeated. 'What can happen?'

Anne's mouth tightened. Once more she glanced down at her right hand.

'I don't know,' she answered, speaking half to herself in a sort of anguish. 'I don't know. If only I did!'

'If you'd tell me the truth,' I said quietly, 'I'm sure I could help you.'

'Oh Margaret, if only you *could* help me!' Anne cried out. 'If only you could!'

Suddenly Anne broke down and began to cry with long racking sobs. I went across to her and put my arm around her. I could only think of trite words to say.

'Don't cry, Anne,' I muttered. 'Please don't cry. Nothing in life is as terrible as we think it's going to be.'

'Don't take any notice of me,' Anne said in a muffled voice. 'I'm just tired that's all. I can't sleep. Tom's really sweet to me, and it worries him that I stay awake all night so he's taken to sleeping in his dressing-room. Sometimes I doze off for a little. But it's never for long. And I just lie there, waiting. And I hear the clock on the landing, tolling out each hour.'

'You lie waiting for what?'

'I don't know, Margaret,' Anne murmured through her tears. 'Perhaps I'm not waiting for anything.'

Her sobs grew more violent. I began to stroke her hair.

'Tell me what you are waiting for,' I insisted.

'I've told you,' Anne answered. 'I don't know. I don't know, I promise you.'

'You must tell me,' I replied.

'There's nothing,' Anne gasped out. 'There's nothing at all. Please leave me alone. I'm fond of you, Margaret. But you must leave me to myself. You must leave me alone. You must. Really you must.'

Still sobbing, Anne got up from her chair and left me.

22

Never have I known Tom so gentle or Margaret so kind as each of them has been during the last seven weeks. I am sincerely grateful to them. I know that I don't deserve such consideration. But, of course, their solicitude will make my final departure all the more difficult. Indeed, I sometimes feel that I am in danger of being imprisoned by their warmth and tenderness. But nothing has changed my resolve to join Sunil. Certainly, I was not swayed by the warning that Rodney Meadows gave me about what my life might be like in Ceylon. I am very sad when I think of Rodney's loneliness. But I still have the sense to realise that all he said about the difficulties of living with Sunil in his home village was inspired by jealousy. And I was greatly disturbed by his final outburst. So I have decided I will not visit his bungalow again. Meanwhile, I have made all the preparations that I can for my departure. The main reason I did not leave immediately with Sunil was because I did not wish to leave Tom and Margaret like a cowardly deserter. The other night when I broke down and cried in front of Margaret I had already gone as far as I dared in warning her that I would soon be leaving. I have written a farewell letter to Tom which I have concealed beneath the paper at the bottom of my wardrobe in our bedroom and which I will leave on my dressing-table the night that I go away.

'Dear Tom,' I wrote. 'When you wake up in the morning and leave your dressing-room and come into our bedroom you will find this letter. By that time I will have left this country. You may guess where I have gone and what made me decide to go. You will be very angry with me, and you will despise me. If only you knew what agony of mind I have gone through and how hard it has been for me to make this decision.

'I am very much aware how disloyally I have behaved. I have deserted you and I have betrayed you. But please, Tom, please believe me when I tell you that when you came to my parents' house and asked me to marry you, I sincerely thought I was very much in love with you. And when I accepted your proposal of marriage I was certain that I could make you a loyal and loving wife. But, as we all know, we cannot control the inclinations of our hearts, or the desires of our bodies—unless we be possessed of exceptional moral righteousness which, alas, I am not. I tried to force myself to love you, but it was all in vain. Then, in Sunil, I found a boy of roughly my own age with whom despite myself I fell hopelessly and passionately in love.

'I now love him so intensely that I think of him every single moment of every single day. He is my love; he fills my whole existence with his beauty. I can see his reflection in every object I look at. He is in the flowers on the lawn and the cedars of the forest; he is in the glass from which I drink and he is on every page of every book that I read. Sunil is all around me and within me. Yet I know that I am only observing his shadow. It is the reality of his presence for which I crave more intensely with each day that passes by. For I cannot live with only the shadow of my love. So I must go to him. And this means that I must leave you and Margaret for ever.

'By the time you get this letter, Sunil will have sent for me, and I will be crossing the straits to join him in the home he has made for us.

'Please, Tom, I beseech you, please do not make any attempt to find me. Whatever happens, I can never return again to Mickleden. I will have crossed the barrier. I may be making a mistake. But I would rather be mistaken and know once more the ecstasy of love than live in rectitude and loneliness of spirit for the rest of my life.

'I do pray that you and Margaret will in time forgive me. And forgive my disloyalty. Please give my love to Margaret.

I respect her and I am fond of her. Thank you both for all your kindness and for all your patience with me. I am very conscious of the fact that essentially, Tom, you are a good and generous-minded man. You deserve a far better wife than I could ever be. I only hope that in the course of time you will find one. Please try to put me out of your mind for always. Please think of me as being of no more importance than a short interlude in your life.'

❖

I have packed a small bag. I have concealed it in a corner of a disused cupboard on the landing outside our bedroom. Into it I have put such personal belongings as I will need, together with the few pieces of jewellery I possess so that Sunil can sell them and raise money.

I am prepared for the journey. I had considered writing a letter to my parents. Indeed I wrote three different draughts but I burned each one of them. I found the task too painful and difficult; I have given up the attempt.

Because I am so restless at night nowadays, Tom always sleeps in his dressing-room. He drinks heavily each evening, and he sleeps soundly. The actual problem of leaving the house silently without awakening anyone will not be difficult. I have discovered each one of the stairs that creaks, and I know which side to walk on without making a sound. I am ready.

But why doesn't the guide arrive? As I look out through the window in front of my desk, why do I not see a strip of blue cloth tied to the weather-cock as it veers with the winds? What has happened? Sunil promised that the guide would arrive within three weeks. 'Perhaps three weeks, no more.' Those were his very words. I can remember them clearly. So what could have occurred to upset Sunil's plan? Is it possible that he has not managed to make contact with the guide, his cousin in Dhanuskode? Or did the guide arrive here one evening and could not climb over the compound wall? Or has Tom been lying to me and did he catch Sunil before he reached the straits, and is Sunil now in some remote prison? But each time I ask myself this, I end by refusing to believe that Tom would lie to me. So what is the explanation? As each day passes, I cannot help being tortured by ghastly possibilities. Perhaps Sunil was thrown at the moment the chestnut gelding was lamed. Perhaps he has broken a leg. Perhaps he is in some hospital in Ceylon or in hiding in the village of Dhanuskode. Perhaps, as he crossed the straits, a storm broke out and the little boat was swept away into the ocean and foundered in the waves. My imagination supplies me daily with a seemingly endless series of reasons for the delay.

I have been so distracted by uncertainty during these last few days that I have even considered asking Tom if I could make a journey to the village of Dhanuskode. Somehow I might be able to make contact with Sunil's cousin who lives there, though I do not know his name. But Tom might suspect the reason for my eagerness to visit the village.

I do not think I can bear my anxiety of mind much longer. Already, I am aware that my behaviour has grown strange. I have now almost managed to convince myself that Sunil is waiting for the next full moon. So, in a way, I have become less afraid. But I notice that Tom and Margaret have taken to watching me covertly. The other day, for instance, Margaret suddenly asked me if my hand was hurting, and I realised that I must have been gazing down at my hand for some time. I was thinking of that last afternoon in the glade when Sunil kissed the palm of my right hand. 'Let your right hand remember my kiss until we meet again,' he had said. Margaret is very gentle and understanding. Sometimes I wonder if she has discovered the truth. But if she has found out my secret, I am certain that she has not told Tom. I feel guilty because I know I am hurting Tom by my apathy. I turn and find him staring at me with a kind of perplexed expression. My final departure may come as a blessing to him, for then he will be able to forget me for good and all.

◄◄◆►►

I have just gone to the window and stared out. For an instant I thought I could see a thin strip of blue cloth fluttering in the

170

breeze. But once again it was my imagination. I now limit the number of occasions I allow myself to look out of the window to six times a day. It is very hard to keep to this rule, and sometimes I cheat. Each time I find there is no strip of cloth, I am filled with a cold despair. In my hopelessness I even allow myself to contemplate the prospect that the guide will never appear, I begin to be afraid that now he is in Ceylon Sunil has decided to forget about me. Then I look down at the palm of my hand and I remember his kiss, and I remember the intensity of his hoarse voice. 'Anne, never forget,' he told me. 'Know that in your right hand lies Sunil's heart and soul.' So I must have faith in him. There must be some reason for this delay which I shall learn in due course. Meanwhile, I must remain confident that at any moment the guide will arrive and I will be taken to my darling one. Yen anbé.

It is time for me to go to the window and look out once again.

23

I am not a man to worry unduly, but I cannot help being concerned about Anne. She remains for hours in her sitting-room, staring down at her desk and sometimes gazing out of the window, neither reading nor writing. She refuses to go out riding any more. She seldom leaves the house. Sometimes she will take the carriage to drive to the library, and sometimes I can persuade her to accompany Margaret when she goes shopping. But Anne now appears to grudge every moment she spends away from the house. Occasionally she will take a walk round the garden, but she rarely bothers to look at the banks of flowers that Margaret has planted with such care.

When I think about Margaret I am reminded of my second worry. I am aware that I am not an intelligent man. However, I do possess a certain intuition, and for reasons I cannot explain I have had a feeling that there now exists some kind of understanding between Margaret and Anne. I know that it is not unusual for two women in a house to share trivial little secrets which they can discuss in private and which afford them some solidarity in confronting any male members of the household. But knowing Margaret's character, I do not think that she would lend herself to such a silly form of behaviour. Whatever understanding there is between Margaret and Anne goes far deeper. Moreover, my instinct tells me that there is some matter which is being deliberately withheld from me. I have trusted Margaret since I was a child, so it has grieved me to suspect that she has been keeping secret from me something of concern.

Yesterday I decided to tackle her on the matter as soon as we were left alone.

'Margaret,' I said to her, 'as you well know, I am extremely worried about Anne. She seems to be growing more distracted every day. And if she continues to lose weight, she will become emaciated. I have an odd feeling that you know the reason for her distress. Is that true?'

Margaret folded the newpaper she had been reading and laid it on the table beside her. Then she looked up at me composedly.

'Why should you think I know the reason?' she asked.

'I've watched the two of you together,' I said. 'I've seen the glances you give each other. Sometimes I believe that you share some important secret.'

Margaret's mouth gave a slight twitch, but she still gazed at me calmly. I was determined to break down her resistance.

'Sometimes you look like a couple of conspirators,' I told her. 'What have you conspired about? Is it a conspiracy against me?'

'You've let your imagination run away with you,' Margaret answered. 'You know that I would never conspire against you. The idea of it is preposterous.'

'Then what is the secret?' I insisted.

'Let me tell you this,' Margaret replied. 'If I knew the reason for Anne's ill state of mind, I would tell you immediately, I promise you. But I don't.'

'But you share a secret just the same,' I stated.

'Of course we do,' Margaret answered placidly. 'I've grown really fond of Anne, and I think she's now taken to me. And all over the world women who are friends in the same house *do* share secrets. Sometimes several. And that's all there is to it.'

With that answer I had to be content. But I was left with the same feeling of resentment which I used to experience in the nursery when Margaret, who had appeared to be losing, would win a game of draughts by an adroit skilful move.

'May I give you a piece of advice?' Margaret asked suddenly.

'Certainly.'

'Put this stupid idea of a conspiracy right out of your mind,' Margaret said. 'Already Anne suffers from the delusion that you and I spy on her. If you go to her and accuse her of conspiring with me against you it's only going to make matters worse.'

Margaret stood up and adjusted the folds of her skirt with a gesture that I remembered so well.

'May I ask you a very personal question?' she enquired.

'Yes.'

'You told me recently that you now sleep most nights in your dressing-room,' Margaret said. 'Do you never go into Anne's room?'

I understood the meaning behind Margaret's words.

'Very seldom,' I answered.

'Then I suggest you may be making a mistake,' Margaret told me. 'I may be wrong. Obviously, I'd never discuss such a thing with Anne. But I believe that it might be a good idea to renew your attentions. I know you love her very much. Prove it to her.'

———✦———

I was by no means sure about the wisdom of Margaret's advice at the end of my rather unsatisfactory conversation with her. However, in any case that evening a game of *Chemin de fer* had been arranged at the Mess, and I had promised to attend. After dinner the long table was cleared, and we sat down to play. I drew lucky cards, and though I wanted to go home early, I did not like to leave while I was winning money. It was past midnight by the time I decided that I could decently retire from the game. As I rode up to Mickleden I saw that the house was in darkness except for a light in our bedroom window which streamed out through the partly drawn curtains. Perhaps Anne had fallen asleep while reading. I dismounted. Doshan took the reins from my hands and I bade him good-night. As usual, I greeted the night-watchman; I went into the house, picked up a lamp in the hall and walked upstairs. For once I was almost completely sober, because I had become so absorbed by the game that I had forgotten to drink.

I opened the door of our bedroom. To my surprise I saw

Anne in her nightgown standing at the curtain beside her dressing-table. She appeared to be gazing out at the night. As I closed the door, Anne turned round and took a few paces towards me. The expression of her face had changed so much that for an instant I had the shock of thinking I was looking at a stranger. All the sadness had left her features. She looked like the young girl I used to visit in the farmhouse on my father's estate. Yet not only had the glow of childhood returned to Anne, but her whole being seemed transformed by a fantastic joy. Her countenance appeared to radiate an intense happiness so powerful that I could almost sense its brilliance. This transformation made her look more lovely than I had ever known her. She was now standing facing me, but in a curious way her eyes were not seeing me, nor did she give the impression of being aware of my presence.

Suddenly I became suspicious. Why had she been staring out of the window? What had been responsible for this blaze of happiness? I went to the window and looked out. A full moon was shining down on to the yard. No one was about. The yard was completely empty. The night-watchman must be on his patrol on the other side of the house. There was not a sound. The stable-doors were closed. I could see nothing unusual—nothing to account for Anne to be standing by the curtains, nothing to explain her present radiance. Perhaps, inexplicably, the terrible depression had lifted from Anne's mind, and she had been standing at the window, gazing out at the full moon and thanking Providence for her recovery.

As I moved away from the window, Anne seemed to come out of her trance. She became aware of my presence and smiled at me.

'Did you have a good evening?' she asked.

'Yes,' I answered. 'Excellent.'

'Did you win?' Anne enquired.

'A little,' I replied.

'I'm glad you won,' Anne said.

'Thank you,' I answered.

'I'm glad,' Anne repeated.

There was silence. Anne was watching me carefully. I had

an odd impression that she expected me to make some move or to deliver some utterance. Then I remembered Margaret's advice. At the same time, as I looked at Anne, I realised with a quick stab of passion how very beautiful she was and how much I desired her. I had never wanted her so fiercely as I did at that moment. I could feel the force of my desire welling up in me. I went across to Anne and stood in front of her. Slowly I raised my hand and began to stroke her cheek. Anne smiled at me. I could feel the warmth of her body beneath her nightgown. When I drew her towards the bed she made no resistance. Quickly I took off my clothes. I removed her gown. For a moment I stood gazing at her nakedness. Then I lay down beside her and began to fondle her breasts. Anne gave a little shiver. The look of contentment was still on her face. As my hands moved over her body she began to tremble. She was breathing rapidly. Her lips were parted. When I pressed into her she gave a short cry, and I could feel her hands clasping my back. For the first time she was wild in her passion. She had reached a state of ecstasy. Her arms were clutching me to her as if she would never let me go. When the climax came she gave a long moan. Presently we were lying peacefully together with our limbs still entwined. I was filled with happiness because Anne had at last showed that she loved me.

'Shall I stay the night?' I whispered to her.

Anne looked at me in silence. Suddenly her expression changed, and she stared at me in surprise, as if I were a stranger.

'What is it?' I asked. 'What's wrong?'

'Nothing,' Anne answered. 'Nothing, I promise you.'

'Then shall I sleep here tonight?'

'I'm afraid I will be restless,' Anne answered. 'I've been restless all evening. That's why you found me out of bed when you came in. I had tried to sleep, but I couldn't. So if you don't mind, Tom, I think you'd better sleep tonight in your dressing-room.'

'Very well,' I replied. Gently I kissed her forehead. 'Oh, my darling Anne,' I murmured. 'I'm so happy. You've made me wonderfully happy. And I love you very much. And I always will love you, my little darling. I'll love you.'

As I spoke, I could see Anne's lips begin to quiver, and for a moment I was afraid she was going to cry. With a strange gasp she covered her face with her hands.

'Thank you, Tom,' she said in a muffled voice. 'Thank you for your kindness. Thank you for everything.'

Once again I kissed her forehead. I got out of bed. I decided to collect my clothes in the morning. I took up the lamp I had brought with me.

'Bless you,' I said. 'Try to get some sleep. Good-night, my darling.'

I walked into my dressing-room and closed the door behind me. I knew I would sleep well.

24

After the door had closed behind him, I waited for a while in case he should return for his clothes. Then I rose and went to the window. I wanted to reassure myself that what I had seen had not been a dream. I looked out. It was a clear night, and the moon was full. I could see each stone in the yard. I could feel my heart beating as I raised my head. The weather-cock glittered in the moonlight, and tied to it was a thin strip of blue cloth which waved in the slight breeze. The signal was there at last. I stood motionless, fixing my gaze on it. I had not been dreaming. But seeing the blue strip of cloth after waiting for so long had given me a shock. And I had been in a daze when Tom came back from playing cards. In this confusion, I had let him make love to me, and my mind had been so full of Sunil that while Tom embraced me I had imagined that it was Sunil whose arms were holding me and whose body was joined with mine, and I had experienced the joy of reunion with him.

I was still dazed, but I knew I must make an effort to move away from the window and to put my plan into action. I turned away and glanced at the clock on the bedside table. It was nearly two. I must be quick. The guide would be waiting for me. Once more I stared out of the window. The strip of cloth was now fluttering proudly from its mast, but a faint mist had covered the yard.

I have managed to leave the window.

I have put on my clothes without making a sound. The house

is so silent tonight that even through the thickness of the dressing-room door I can hear the sound of Tom's snoring. I take out the envelope from beneath the paper at the bottom of my wardrobe. I place it on the dressing-room table so that Tom will find it when he comes to collect his clothes in the morning. By the time he reads my farewell letter I will be crossing the straits. Then I hesitate. What if Tom should come into the bedroom for some reason in the early hours of the morning and find the letter before I have reached the fishing-village? If he comes in and finds I have gone, he may suspect I am heading for Dhanuskode, but he will not be certain. Therefore, surely it would be wiser to leave the letter in some place where he will not find it immediately? I decide this plan is safer. So I slide the letter under a book—an anthology of poetry which always lies on my bedside table. Eventually it will be discovered. I take a last look around the room—the room in which my marriage in effect began and has now ended. There is nothing I have forgotten. I blow out the lamp by my bedside. I can see my way by the light of the moon shining through the gap in the curtains. I go to the door and open it. Moonlight flows on to the landing from a fan-light above the passage. Carefully I open the disused cupboard and take out the small leather bag I have packed. Then I begin to move cautiously down the staircase, avoiding parts of the steps that creak. I walk silently along the hall. Softly I open the front door a few inches and peer out. The ground mist has become a little thicker. I see the night-watchman moving away from the porte-cochère. I know that he will be making his way towards the kitchen and the servants' quarters at the back of the house. This is my opportunity. Keeping to the grass verge beside the gravel drive, and passing beneath the palm-trees, I cross the garden and reach the compound gate. I walk through the gate and turn to the right. I am now hidden from view by the height of the compound wall. I follow the wall until I come to the back of the stables. This is the place where the guide must have climbed in to fix the strip of cloth on to the weather-cock. Close by is a small thicket. Beneath these trees the guide will be waiting for me. I walk forward. I can feel my heart thudding with my excitement, but I am not afraid. I move towards a gap in the trees which grow so thickly that the moonlight cannot penetrate. I walk along a narrow path. Then, through the mist, I see the guide and the two horses. He is mounted on a tall grey, and holds the reins of a white horse which looks ghostly in the obscure light. The guide watches me approaching and raises his hand in greeting. I come close to him. For a second I gape, because I believe it is Sunil. Then I realise that the man is far older. His face is lined and his hair is grizzled, but there is still a look of Sunil about him. Silently he dismounts, looping the reins over his arm. He helps me into the saddle. Still in silence, he climbs back on to his own horse, and gestures to me to follow him as he sets off through the thicket. Presently we reach open ground, and the horses canter across the green turf that leads to the wood through which Sunil and I have ridden so often. It is now safe to speak.

'We are riding to Dhanuskode?' I ask.

The guide nods his head.

'Dhanuskode,' he answers.

'I believe it takes less than four hours to cross the straits,' I continue.

'Dhanuskode,' the guide repeats.

I realise that he does not speak English. I examine his face as we ride side by side through the wood. It is a worn face, and the expression is sad. But somehow I trust my guide completely.

Soon we reach the lovely glade in the wood, which holds such intense memories for me. I look at the bank where Sunil first made love to me. I stare at the corner beneath the tall trees where we said good-bye. I have never visited this place since that day. But it no longer has any power to wound me. For as we move across the glade, now dappled with moonlight, I know that with each step of my horse I am moving closer to Sunil. I remember Sunil lying asleep in my arms on the afternoon of that fatal day when we were discovered. I remember a few lines of the sonnet I had begun in that moment of repose as I looked down at the marks of Kumar's whip on Sunil's back.

See the spilt blood is drying in the sun.
  The great weals change to living flesh again,
  But your deep wound has not been made in vain.
Is this the way fulfilment has begun?

As we begin to descend towards the coast the mist grows
thicker so that the rays of the moon are now diffused. The
going becomes difficult so the guide leads the way. My horse is
nimble and footsure; I have nothing to do except follow my
guide. Unexpectedly the mist begins to lift and, by the wavering
light of the moon, suddenly in the far distance I can glimpse a
long stretch of water, calm and unruffled. The straits lie before
us. The guide turns to me and smiles when he sees the look of
happiness on my face.

I can feel the air growing warmer, and I loosen the collar
of my riding-habit. I know that it will be hot where Sunil
lives, so I've packed in my bag two of the light dresses that I
wore in Madras. At last we reach the plain. The horses begin to
canter through the scrub. The sky is growing lighter. Dawn
will soon be breaking. And soon after dawn, Tom will awake
and find that I have gone. But I am a long way ahead of him,
and how can he be certain where I am going? I have no fear of
Tom catching me now.

Ahead of us lies the fishing-village. I can see an assembly of
small whitewashed mud-huts. The guide leads the way to a
narrow jetty. Tied up to the jetty is a fishing-boat, perhaps
thirty feet long. The guide stops and helps me to dismount. He
tethers the two horses. He leads the way along the jetty,
carrying my leather bag. He pauses beside the boat with its
slim outrigger. He calls out softly in Tamil. A wizened Indian
wearing a white turban and a loin-cloth appears on deck. He
sees me and nods his head. Behind him appear two young boys
who are probably his children. The guide motions me to cross
the little gang-plank. As I come on board, the Indian and the
two children salaam. The guide, who now stands beside me,
points at a mattress strewn with pillows on the deck. Then he
turns to go. I take some money out of my bag and offer it to
him, but he refuses vigorously. He salaams in farewell. I can

only smile at him in gratitude. The guide disappears along the jetty. To the east, the sky is flaming with the light of dawn.

One of the boys unties the boat, while the other boy helps the wizened-looking Indian, who is evidently the captain of the ship, to hoist the sail. There is a faint breeze. The boat glides out of the harbour and begins to cross the smooth misty water. I have left India for good. I have left my past life behind. I have escaped from Tom forever. I am free. In a few hours' time I shall see my darling Sunil. I shall feel his tender skin against my lips. I do not know how far it will be from the harbour in Ceylon to Sunil's home. But I shall not mind the length of the journey because I shall be with Sunil. And we shall be alone together. The last part of my sonnet now comes into my mind.

> For we are free now. Never more I'll hear
> The march of feet upon the barrack square.
> Away with slavery, away with fear!
> Never on me the tragic face will stare.
> Home, honour, parents, England, all farewell
> For where my love is, there with love I dwell.

I am tired after the long ride. I smile at the Indian who is at the tiller, and he smiles back. His teeth are black and uneven, but his smile is friendly and reassuring. I cross over to the mattress; I take off the jacket of my riding-habit and lie down. I close my eyes. I can hear the water rippling against the side of the boat. As I lie there, I realise that I am floating between two worlds—the world of my childhood and upbringing and marriage, and the world of my future life with Sunil. Odd scenes flick like lantern-slides across my mind. I am sitting on a bench on the lawn in front of the old farmhouse; Tom is bending over my hand and kissing it. Now, I am coming out of Telacamund church, leaning on Tom's arm; the sunshine glitters on the trumpets of the regimental band. Next, Margaret is sitting beside me as we drive through the streets of Telacamund, passing naked children with crimson sores who are playing in the dust. Marjorie Russell, shapely and provocative, champagne-glass in hand, is talking animatedly to the Rajah; the jewels flash on his fingers. The images continue. Margaret sits alone at the solitaire board in the drawing-room of Mickleden; moths are fluttering round the lamps. Tom stands proudly on the saluting base on the barrack square; two columns of men march past him, their black faces gleaming. Sunil's wrists are tied to rings on the stableyard wall; Kumar raises his whip. Rodney Meadows is leaning against the back of an armchair in his bungalow, glaring at me; a silk handkerchief is clenched in his hand. I am kneeling in a pew in the church at Telacamund; Tom is on one side of me and Margaret is on the other; the shape of the head of the tallest choirboy reminds me of Sunil. I am lying alone and naked on the bank of grass in the glade; a black snake is sliding towards me; a pale light glimmers on the length of it.

I have been dozing. For a moment, when I open my eyes, I do not know where I am. Then I see the captain at the tiller and the two boys crouching beside him. Once again, he smiles at me. The sun is slanting across the tranquil sea. I get up from the mattress. To the south I can discern the outlines of a harbour. We are drawing close to Ceylon. From my bag I take out a hand-mirror and a comb to arrange my hair so that I will look my best when Sunil meets me. I pack my jacket. The boat glides through the entrance of the harbour. I can observe a jetty, with a cluster of houses behind it. As we come closer, I see—to my dismay— that the jetty is deserted. I turn towards the captain enquiringly. Once more, he smiles at me. The two boys lower the sail. The captain steers the boat alongside the jetty. The boys tie up to bollards; then they secure the little gang-plank. The captain takes my bag and steps ashore. I follow him.

Suddenly, at the far end of the jetty, I see a small figure. Instinctively I know that it is Sunil. He is naked except for a sarong around his narrow waist. I begin to run towards him. At that instant he recognises me. He starts to rush towards me. I know that in a moment he will be in my arms. My heart thuds violently. I am still running. I can now distinguish his features.

His lips are parted and his eyes are blazing with happiness. He looks even more beautiful than I remember. All the anguish I have suffered now seems worthwhile for the sake of this young god of loveliness. I am drawing nearer to him.

Then I stumble.

I stumble and fall. I can feel the pain of my fall, but I can see nothing. Darkness is all around. Vaguely I am aware that I am being helped to my feet. I feel muzziness in my head. Why did I hear the sound of glass breaking when I fell? In vain, I try to peer through the dark mist surrounding me. The arms that are holding me are strong. Perhaps it was Sunil who raised me from the ground. Then from far away I can hear a man's voice.

'Anne,' the voice says. 'What's wrong? Tell me what's wrong?'

But it is not Sunil who is speaking to me. It is Tom's voice. So I must have fallen asleep in the boat. I must still be dreaming. But I must now wake up, for the boat is approaching land. Yet I can feel my eyes are open, though I can see nothing.

'Tell me what's wrong,' the voice repeats. 'Why have you been standing all this time by the window? Why haven't you gone to bed?'

I was tired, I know it. The journey to the coast exhausted me. I have fallen into a dream-like state, close to a trance. Surely the captain will wake me before we reach the harbour? He must know that I am meeting Sunil. The arms that are holding me are now shaking me very gently, and gradually the black mist is clearing.

'Don't be frightened,' the voice says. 'You fainted, and you had a fall.'

Dimly through the swirling mist I can see the stableyard. But I have left Mickleden. Eight hours ago I left. So why should each detail of the yard be growing clearer before my eyes? Or is this all part of my dream? I am beginning to be afraid. I can feel myself shivering.

'Don't be distressed,' the voice says quietly. 'You fainted, that's all.'

In my dream—for it must be a dream—I turn my head and

see that it is Tom who is holding me. Drowsily I smile up at him, for now I have no fear of him or resentment. He is looking down at me with a worried expression which somehow disturbs me, and I turn away my head and gaze once more at the yard which is now quite clear in my vision.

'What is it you keep staring at?' Tom asks.

But I must not tell him about the strip of cloth I can see tied to the weather-cock, for if I told him my secret he might pursue me and try to take me home.

'There's nothing,' I reply.

As I become more aware of the pain in my side, and as I begin to see my surroundings with greater clarity, my bewilderment and fear increase. For I begin to doubt that I am dreaming. My pain is very real, the shape of the furniture in the bedroom is very distinct, and I notice that the looking-glass on my dressing-table has fallen down and is broken.

Suddenly, with a lurch of horror, I realise what has happened. I am still standing by the curtains; I have not left the window. My journey to the fishing-village and to the harbour in Ceylon and my meeting with Sunil must all have been part of a dream I had while I stood by the window. I have never even left the room. I must have been in a complete trance. I must have fallen because my legs gave way with fatigue, and I knocked over the looking-glass; that is how it came to be broken. And now that the daylight has come I have lost my opportunity. I have left my departure until too late. When dawn came the guide must have left. In despair I understand what will happen. The guide will return to Dhanuskode without me. Sunil will wait on the jetty for a ship that will never come—or, if it appears, will not bring me to him. And what can he suppose—except that I have changed my mind and no longer love him? And now the moment has passed forever. I do not know how to reach him. I can never let him know the truth. All his life Sunil will believe that I did not love him. He will never be aware of the long weeks of misery I endured while I was waiting for his sign. Yet I can see him so clearly as he ran along the jetty; I can see the blue sarong around his small waist; I can see the light glittering on his ebony-smooth shoulders; I can see the whiteness of his teeth as he smiled and the ecstasy glowing from his face. I have betrayed him; I have betrayed my young god, my lovely one.

Because I am ineffectual—as Rodney told me—I must suffer, I know it. But I have also caused others to suffer. This must certainly change. All that is left to me now is to order my life, if possible, so that I never again cause suffering to any other person. Therefore—so long as he needs me—I must not leave Tom, and I must try to avoid making him or Margaret unhappy.

'Anne, you must leave the window,' Tom says very softly. 'You must go to bed and rest.'

I take one last look at the weather-cock. The breeze has dropped; the strip of cloth hangs limply. Like myself, it will stay here until it rots in the Indian sun.

The Five Sonnets

by

JOHN BETJEMAN

I

<hr/>

Blow winds about the house, you cannot shake me,
    However blustering or strong you blow!
March military feet, you will not wake me
    However loud you trample to and fro!
Go, grim command rapped out, you cannot make me
    Do what I would not. This alone I know,
An inward restlessness will not forsake me,
    A restlessness that does not let me go.

Day after day I feel my body tingling.
    Night after night I hope that, far or near,
Some being waits whose soul with mine commingling
    Will fill the emptiness I suffer here.
I yearn for love, deep, tender, trusting, steady,
Oh unknown lover, now my heart is ready.

2

It must be breakfast time at home today,
    Mamma will give her order to the cook,
    Papa is in his study with his book,
And in the stableyard my dapple grey
Leans over from her box as if to say
    'Where is my mistress?' That farewell I took
    Kissing your muzzle was our last long look.
Old friend, your mistress now is far away.

I married him as if by Royal decree,
Good regiment, a baronet-to-be,
    Rich and a gentleman, they asked no more.
They did not say his liquor-scented breath
And night embraces would be worse than death,
    Nor when he slept, how loudly he would snore.

3

Adultery! The moon and stars permitted it.
　　Adultery! I'm numbered with the thieves.
Adultery, and it was I committed it
　　I hear it in the whisper of the leaves.
The servants creep about, their looks are sidelong
　　They seem to spy on everything I do,
And sense that one who has not been a bride long
　　Already to their master is untrue.

Women at parties seem about to utter,
　　See me and stop; while underneath the stars
Men on verandahs lower their tones and mutter
　　And soon we'll be the talk of the bazaars.
Let them go on with their malicious chatter
Our love, our sacred love alone will matter.

4

Now is my heart on fire, which once was chilled,
   Now are our bodies one which once were two,
   For you are part of me and I of you.
Oh deep strong calm when turbulence is stilled,
In this sweet union which God has willed.
      Come closer, rest, I tremble through and through,
      All you can want of me I gladly do,
Now is the purpose of our lives fulfilled.

Is He not good, God who such rapture gives?
      Such overflowing ecstasy of joy.
Touch, let me touch your warm enticing skin
That I may know my lover breathes and lives.
      My own, my darling sunkiss'd supple boy
If this is sinful, what is wrong with sin?

5

Now has the utmost cruelty been done!
　　Oh, my own darling could I take your pain,
　　And share it with you! Let the heavens rain
Healing upon my wounded lovely one.
See the spilt blood is drying in the sun.
　　The great weals change to living flesh again,
　　But your deep wound has not been made in vain.
Is this the way fulfilment has begun?

For we are free now. Never more I'll hear
　　The march of feet upon the barrack square.
Away with slavery, away with fear!
　　Never on me the tragic face will stare.
Home, honour, parents, England, all farewell
For where my love is, there with love I dwell.